Gravity

....

Leslie Porter

Copyright © 2024 by Leslie Porter

All rights reserved.

No portion of this book may be reproduced in any form without written permission from the publisher or author, except as permitted by U.S. copyright law.

Contents

----

1. Chapter 1 - The Dream — 1
2. Chapter 2 - The Stars — 7
3. Chapter 3 - The First Move — 15
4. Chapter 4 - The Kiss — 20
5. Chapter 5 - The Arrival — 28
6. Chapter 6 - The Friend — 36
7. Chapter 7 - The Special Person — 41
8. Chapter 8 - The Rules — 49
9. Chapter 9 - The Sunset — 53
10. Chapter 10 - The Lab Rat — 62
11. Chapter 11 - The Experiment — 72
12. Chapter 12 - The Kikorangi — 77
13. Chapter 13 - The Vacillator — 84
14. Chapter 14 - The Distraction — 93
15. Chapter 15 - The Black Sheep — 100

16. Chapter 16 - The Peacock   109
17. Chapter 17 - The Decision   117
18. Chapter 18 - The Plan   128
19. Chapter 19 - The Reflection   134
20. Chapter 20 - The Anger   139
21. Chapter 21 - The Truth   146

Chapter 1 - The Dream

"Keep still." The doctor's needle pierced my arm and slipped under the skin, red liquid slowly filling the syringe. Seconds later, the needle was withdrawn and replaced with cotton wool for me to hold onto my arm.

I recalled the day the doctors brought me to this medical facility. I'd been fifteen years old and I'd been practising some daring stunts with friends on our hoverboards. I'd flipped the board over the central ring, lost balance and fallen off, breaking my arm. Breaking my arm had been annoying, but the reason I'd been taken to hospital was because I'd also hit my head, and despite it being covered by a helmet, the angle I'd fallen at had meant that I'd created a wound that had been bleeding.

I'd been rushed to the nearest hospital after one of my friends called for an ambulance, and I remember the concerned look that my Mum had worn as she burst through the door to my hospital room. The doctors had taken good care of me, and had reassured me I would be all right, but the worry had still been etched into her features.

I'd tried to reassure her that the injury looked worse than it really was, and that I'd be out in a few hours. I hadn't seen what all the fuss was about.

Teenage boys had accidents like this all the time. I'd assumed Mum was overreacting, although I knew it could have been partly because she didn't like hospitals and we'd managed to stay away from them until my accident.

Shortly afterwards, one of the medical team had come into the hospital room and told us they'd found an anomaly in my blood that needed investigating. I hadn't really known what that meant.

It turned out it meant I needed to be quarantined in a medical research facility on Selenia, one of the moons of a planet called Omega 6 that I'd never heard of before that day.

That was three years ago, and I'd been here ever since. For my own safety apparently, even though I'd been perfectly fine living on Earth with my mother up until that point. I couldn't understand why my safety was suddenly in question now. Nobody seemed to be able to quite explain to me what I was doing here, other than this blood anomaly. The doctors and scientists in their bright white lab coats had said they would let me know when they had answers.

In the meantime, I was well looked after. I had access to books, films and games, and my Mum visited me every day. I taught myself how to pilot different types of spacecraft from flight manuals and simulations, in the hope that one day I might actually get to fly one.

But still, they couldn't give me the one thing I wanted more than anything. To get out of here. To go back home and get on with my life. Freedom. I was so bored with being poked and prodded and tested. With all the physical exercises and measurements of my heart rate and blood pressure. With the blood that got taken from me three times a day. What on earth could they be doing with so many blood samples? "Mr Miller?" A lady's voice brought me back to reality. She was on the other side of the transparent forcefield that kept me in my living area. She was pretty, with strawberry-blonde hair and blue eyes, and her name tag read 'Dr. Milan.' I didn't recognise her, so I assumed she was new.

"Hmmm?" I'd totally missed the question.

"Are you hungry?" she asked, or from her point of view, probably repeated.

"Yeah, I could eat." I smiled at her. "What's on the menu?"

She smiled back. "A little birdy told me you like the burgers."

She wasn't wrong. My smile broadened as I agreed to a burger. The food was good here, at least.

Several minutes later she returned with a large juicy burger, with a side salad. They all knew I was one of the few people that didn't like chips, and they had stopped offering them to me. As soon as the forcefield dropped, the amazing smell of the steaming hot meat and warm bread hit my nose. I thanked her and sat down to eat. Whatever was supposedly wrong with me, it clearly hadn't affected my appetite and the food was gone within minutes.

I pushed my empty plate and cutlery to one side, and that was when he walked around the corner, wearing a white lab coat and standard issue name badge. The man of my dreams. Only, this guy was substantially better than any of the men in the dreams I'd had so far. His dark hair was messy and stopped slightly before it fell into his ocean-blue eyes. He didn't look much older than me, probably early twenties, and his full pink lips parted to speak to Dr Milan, who was only a couple of metres from my forcefield and probably about to take my plate away.

"I'm looking for Damon Miller?" he asked politely, smiling at her with a dimple appearing, and my heart jolted me upright, knocking my chair over as I stood.

Not only was he the most gorgeous creature I had ever set eyes on, but he was looking for me? I wished I had a mirror available to check I looked presentable. I rested back against the table, trying to look casual, despite the chair still lying on the floor.

Judging by the way the strawberry-blonde was tripping over her words and blushing while she directed him to me, apparently, he was the man of her dreams too.

Mr Gorgeous thanked her and took the couple of steps needed to get to the edge of my forcefield.

"Hi Damon," he smiled, and I swear I nearly fainted.

"Hi," I squeaked back, trying to stay casual and failing miserably.

"I just need you to come with me for a couple of tests please?" he said, releasing the forcefield.

Well, this was strange. Not the fact that the medical staff wanted to run tests on me; that part had been fairly standard. But they generally had a timetable and they stuck to it. Taking me for a test straight after dinner had never happened before. However, I'd learned that I didn't really have much say in these matters. Besides, I would get to be alone with – I managed to drag my eyes away from his face long enough to read his name badge – Dr Tarnung.

"Sure," I replied, trying to make my tone lower and more manly than the squeak I gave him before.

In silence, Dr Tarnung led me down various polished white corridors that I'd never been down before, much further than I'd usually go for tests. I had the distinct impression he was concentrating, and I was torn between wanting to talk to him, and not wanting to annoy him by breaking his concentration.

In the end, the temptation to talk to him outweighed anything else.

"So, what are we testing for today?" I ventured.

"Just keep walking please," he replied, but his tone wasn't unpleasant, just firm.

We rounded a corner and were stopped by a short, grey-haired man in the standard uniform. I recognised Dr Firth because he was someone who regularly did my blood tests. He looked between Dr Tarnung and me, and then back to Dr Tarnung again.

"Damon shouldn't be out of his room," Dr Firth said, sounding confused, and then his tone turned suspicious. "What's going on?"

Dr Tarnung seemed to consider his options for a couple of seconds, and then brought his arm back. When his arm shot forward, it was fisted, and connected with the smaller man's chin, sending him flying backwards, dazed.

"Run!" he shouted at me.

Confusion rooted me to the spot. Was this part of the test? I looked at Dr Tarnung, who had started running towards the forcefield at the end of the passageway. He paused only to swipe the scanner that released the forcefield.

"Run!" he repeated, waving to encourage me to move, and this time I obeyed, following him through where the forcefield had been and outside.

Outside? What the hell? I hadn't been outside for the last three years! Why was I outside?

"Get to the ship!" he shouted at me, pointing to the small battered-looking space-craft parked in the fifth docking bay.

That's when I realised I must be dreaming. I was being rescued from my dreary hospital-life by a guy who looked more like a god than a human. Of course this wasn't real. Adrenaline coursed through me, but it was through excitement more than it was through fear. I heard the buzzing of laser-fire from behind as they tried to stop us, which just served to make the dream more exhilarating. I felt light on my feet, like I was part running and part flying.

We made it to the ship – the 'Pavo' according to the letters in faded white written up the side – and like any good dream, the door closed seconds before they could stop us.

"Yes!" I cried out, punching the air like a child.

Although I would probably wake up soon, I intended to enjoy my outdoor adventure for as long as it lasted, even if it was all in my head.

Chapter 2 - The Stars

Dr Tarnung was already at the controls, and I reached out to steady myself as we took off. This was so cool. There was a co-pilot seat next to him, so I aimed towards it, despite the craft rocking back and forth as my companion manoeuvred us away from the firing squad and out of the atmosphere.

"Do you know how to fly?" he asked.

"I've read some manuals and done some simulations, but never actually flown anything," I confessed. "I can probably do the basics with this," I added, looking at the flight controls.

"OK, take the main controls and aim us towards the dwarf star you can see there," he pointed. "I need to make sure nobody's following us."

"You want me to take control?" I quipped, figuring I may as well flirt since I'd be waking up soon anyway, sliding into the black leather chair. "Any time you like."

He got up and pulled on a lever while looking at a colourful display. The dream was already the most realistic and coolest dream I'd ever had, so it was probably asking too much for my brain to get him to flirt back with me.

I heard weapons fire as I pulled the main control stick so that we were facing in the direction he'd instructed me. I assumed he was trying to deter our pursuers from following us.

Dr Tarnung got back into the pilot seat, while Selenia grew smaller in the rear viewer as we pulled away from it. He brought up a scanner and sighed in relief.

"They're not following us for now, but we need to minimise our speed so they can't trace which direction we've gone in." He continued to fiddle with the controls, while I crossed one ankle over another and put my feet up on the dashboard. "If we go too fast, we'll leave an ion trail that they can use to figure out where we are."

I couldn't work out whether he was talking to me or to himself, so I didn't respond until he looked like he'd finished doing whatever he was doing and settled in a bit more.

"So, where are we going?" I asked him.

I was still riding an adrenaline high, and probably grinning insanely.

"Epsilon 4," he responded, taking a deep breath and releasing it slowly.

"What's on Epsilon 4?" I asked.

"Friends and safety," he replied cryptically, removing his lab coat.

"I guess you're not a real doctor, then," I speculated, gesturing towards the lab coat that was being discarded over the back of the pilot's chair. Dr Tarnung was left wearing a vest-top that clung in all the right places. He clearly worked out, but he wasn't overly muscular, and I found it difficult to stop my eyes wandering over his lean, well-toned body.

"Correct," he confirmed.

"So, your name isn't Dr Tarnung?" I asked, pointing to the badge on the discarded lab coat.

"What? Oh, I see. No, my name is Keleon," he smiled over at me. That dimple was back and I couldn't believe how much it affected me.

"I'm Damon," I responded robotically, still checking him out.

"I know," he responded, smile growing.

"Oh, yeah," I realised dumbly.

Of course he knew. I was far too distracted by his beauty to concentrate properly.

"I should send a message to my mother," I said, changing the subject. "Otherwise she'll try to visit me tomorrow."

"If we try to send a message, they'll intercept it and figure out where we are," replied Keleon. "I'm sorry, Damon. Too much time and effort has gone into getting you out of there. We can't risk them finding you. Your mother will understand."

I was slowly starting to realise this wasn't a dream. Everything felt too real. The leather of the seat I was in. The unstable floor as we pulled out of the gravitational field of Selenia. The musty smell in the dated cockpit.

There was too much going on to wrap my head around, so as we sat in comfortable silence, I let my mind wander to things that were simpler than the complex situation I seemed to be in. I wasn't in control of any of this, just like I hadn't been in control of my life for the last three years, so my mind wandered onto things I could perhaps control.

I started to wonder what I should do, if anything, about this instant attraction I had towards Keleon. I had no idea how long the journey to Epsilon 4 would take, or what would happen when we got there. After we arrived, would I ever see him again?

My mother had always told me that we only live once, and we should make the most of every opportunity we could. I knew my dark blonde hair and blue eyes complimented my features because I'd been flirted with by several female members of staff at the medical facility. Which meant that if Keleon was interested in men in any way, I probably stood a chance.

That wasn't something I was going to find out without asking him. If I did nothing, we'd probably part ways without me knowing whether any intimacy with him was possible. But it could be really embarrassing if I started flirting with him and he rejected my advances. He might even be married already. Was it worth the risk?

I looked over at him and drank in his features. My gaze drifted to those perfect pink lips. I really wanted to feel them pressed against mine. I ran my fingers over my bottom lip as I thought about the worst thing that could happen if I made it clear I was interested. He'd reject me, I'd make an idiot of myself, and then I'd probably never see him again. At least I'd know how he felt, and I wouldn't spend my life wondering 'what if?'

Keleon turned to face me and caught me staring. The dimple came back as he smiled. Stunning. I knew I might be being shallow, but yeah, it was worth the risk. It might end in nothing but embarrassment. But who knows, it might result in a kiss that I could remember forever.

"You OK?" he asked.

"I'm good," I replied. "Finding it hard to believe I'm out of that place," I added honestly.

"I'm not surprised, it must have come as a bit of a shock," said Keleon gently. "I wish we'd had some way of letting you know that we were getting you out. Did they treat you well there?"

"Yeah, I guess so. I mean, they poked me and prodded me, but they never really hurt me or anything. The food was good," I added, remembering the burger I had just before I left.

Keleon looked like I'd prompted him to remember something.

"I nearly forgot - there's a bit of food in the back. Do you want some?"

My eyes moved away from his, and I bit my lips as my gaze dropped downwards. I tried to make sure he could see that I was making a point of taking in his beautiful features, my gaze drifting over his body and back up to meet his eyes again.

"Are those two sentences related?" I ventured.

I felt my face heat up slightly, not sure whether that was too forward or not. I was very much out of practice at flirting with anyone I actually wanted to get physical with.

I braced myself for rejection, but he just smiled at me before looking out of the window at the stars.

Out of all the reactions I speculated were possible, a complete lack of reaction wasn't one of them, and I wasn't sure how to interpret it. But damn, he looked hot as he was staring out into the universe. He pushed his hair back away from his eyes, but it just flopped back into the same position and he settled his clasped hands behind his head and put his crossed ankles up on the dash to join mine. He seemed happy to sit in silence, and I was happy to sit and look at him.

"Strange to think that stars are balls of plasma held together by their own gravity," Keleon mused. "There's something majestic about them. Something beyond science. Something ... beautiful."

"I'm definitely enjoying the view," I hinted strongly, with a raised eyebrow.

"That one over there is a Blue Star," he pointed out the window, completely oblivious to the compliment. Either that, or he was ignoring it. "They're quite rare and have relatively short life spans. And normally end very explosively. But in the meantime, very pretty."

I looked out of the window and saw what he meant. A star somewhat larger than those surrounding it and with a blue tint. Keleon was right, it was pretty. As my gaze scanned the sky, I started to notice more and more of the stars, and the patterns they made in the darkness. There was another smaller pretty one tinted red, with a cluster of tiny white ones immediately to the right of it.

"I haven't seen the stars in three years," I realised out loud.

"I can't imagine not seeing the stars for even one year," Keleon replied. "I love being out here, there's nothing quite like it."

I could hear from his tone just how much that was true. And it was easy to see why when I stopped to take it all in.

"What type of star is that one, the one tinted red?" I asked.

I didn't know much about stars, and there was nobody I'd rather learn from.

Two hours later, we were still discussing the different types of stars. Keleon knew so much about dwarf stars, binary stars, supernovas and various other types, and I was very happy to listen to him, feeling a new sense of awe and admiration for my travelling companion.

It felt like only ten minutes had passed since we started talking, so I surprised myself by when I yawned.

"You're tired," said Keleon as he stood up.

He walked towards the back of the small craft and I followed. A side door revealed a small room and he led me inside. He went straight to a panel on the wall and pulled on it. It creaked open, as if it hadn't been used in a while, and he unhooked various pieces of apparatus. The whole thing unfurled into a bed, including a very basic pillow and blanket set. It was smaller than I was used to; the bed I had had in the research facility had been luxurious in comparison. But it was certainly better than sleeping on the floor.

"Thanks," I said, before noticing there was only one bed. I looked back to the man who took my breath away just by being in the same room. "Don't you need to sleep too?"

Keleon smiled and shook his head.

"No. It's all yours."

It made sense that he was on a different sleep-cycle to me. My body clock was still on Selenia time.

I collapsed onto the rickety bed with my hands clasped behind the back of my head. It was so nice to feel cared about. It reminded me of Mum tucking me into my bed when I was a child. Which is possibly what prompted me to ask, "So, do I get a kiss goodnight?"

My cheeks heated but I kept eye contact. Subtle hints had been ignored, so I was going for something a little stronger.

Keleon looked down at me, smiling.

"You're not like the others, Damon. You're perplexing, and you don't make much sense to me. But I like you already. Sleep well."

I was stunned into silence.

Keleon turned and left the small room, closing the door behind him.

I closed my eyes, confusion penetrating every part of my mind. What was it that wasn't making sense to him? It's not like I was being subtle. In fact, I thought I'd been making myself very clear.

Maybe he thought I was joking? Did I need to be even more forward? He was the one not making much sense.

And who were the 'others' I was being compared to?

I turned over and tried to think more positive thoughts. I had longed to get out of that medical facility for the last three years, and now I was free. I didn't feel 'ill' and nobody could tell me what was supposed to be 'wrong' with me, so it seemed like the right time to move on. Hopefully Mum would realise why I didn't contact her, and we'd find each other later. The doctors were bound to get bored of looking for me after a few days. After all, what's the point in trying to treat someone who doesn't want to be treated?

There were more positive thoughts I could focus on too. I had asked Keleon to kiss me, and the result was that he told me he liked me. Although he hadn't acted on my request, and I was left with more questions than answers, it wasn't a rejection.

Those thoughts were enough for hope to swell in my chest as sleep consumed me.

Chapter 3 - The First Move

My body jerked awake as I nearly rolled off the bed. Evidently, I was used to my sleeping area being slightly larger. It felt like I'd slept for hours, and given that the time that had just elapsed would have been a full night on Selenia, it was now probably what would usually be my morning.

The room wasn't much bigger than the bed, so I stood up and poked a couple of the buttons on the wall. One of them released water through a small alcove, large enough for me to put my hand in it.

A dark green folded piece of material lay close by on a raised shelf. I assumed that was what passed as a towel in here. I used the water to wash as much of myself as I could, and the towel to dry off. There was no hairbrush, so I did what I could with the water and my fingers. No mirror either, so I just had to hope I looked reasonable.

I found a box of chewable tablets for cleaning teeth and assumed it would be OK to pinch one. Maybe part of me was being overly optimistic about getting that close to Keleon, but it didn't hurt to be prepared.

I inhaled deeply with anticipation and opened the door that led to the cockpit.

Keleon looked more breathtaking than ever. His ankles were crossed and resting up on the dashboard as he was looking out at the stars, his dark hair resting against his forehead in the sexiest way possible.

"Morning, gorgeous," I offered, leaning against the frame of the entrance to the cockpit.

It was still very forward, but apparently, he needed forward.

"Hi Damon," he greeted as he turned to face me, still seemingly oblivious to my advances. "You must be hungry. There's food in here."

He got up and opened the door opposite the room I'd been sleeping in. I followed.

"There are various different types of ration packs in this room." He gestured to various boxes of ration packs and some bottled water. I knew none of them would be anywhere near as tasty as a burger, but the freedom was worth it.

"Don't you need to eat?" I asked, reaching for one of the packets, and tearing off the foil.

He shook his head.

"No, just take whatever you like."

He must have eaten while I'd been asleep. I took my pack and bottle of water and followed him out into the cockpit to eat.

"How long until we get to Epsilon 4?" I asked between mouthfuls of something stringy that tasted like it was supposed to be meat and failing.

His blue eyes met mine. So unbelievably beautiful.

"Another thirty hours or so. It would normally be faster, but we can't use more than minimum thrust in case they're trying to follow us and detect the ion trail."

"Shame," I replied. "I quite like the idea of experiencing a bit of thrust with you."

As I spoke, I made a point of making sure he could see my eyes roaming over his toned arms, across his covered chest and back up to meet his again. I even threw in a wink at the end of the sentence before disengaging eye contact and taking another bite of my food. Surely, he was receiving the message now. He'd seen the wink; I was sure of it.

His smile widened.

"Do you like chess?" he asked.

Well that was random and unexpected.

"Uh, yeah, I played a few times against the doctors on Selenia," I answered.

"I found a chess set tucked into one of the boxes under the food," he explained. "The previous occupant of this ship must have liked playing. When you've finished eating, would you like a game with me?"

I blinked in astonishment. According to Keleon's observations last night, I was 'perplexing' and 'didn't make much sense.' Yet from my perspective, it was the other way around. He surely must have recognised I was hitting on him, and yet he gave no indication whether I should continue or stop.

I was aware I only had around thirty hours to find out whether my efforts were in vain. I finished my mouthful and asked a random question back, since we seemed to be in that mode.

"Where did you get this ship, anyway? You didn't know the previous occupant?" The last mouthful of whatever I'd been eating went into my mouth, followed by a few large gulps of water from one of the bottles I'd grabbed.

"I borrowed it," he replied, and I raised an eyebrow in response. "With permission," he clarified, apparently being able to decipher what a raised eyebrow in this context meant.

"Right," I drawled. "You want to be black or white?"

"Excuse me?" he asked.

"Chess. Would you rather be black or white?"

"Black," he replied after thinking for a second. "I think I want you to make the first move."

"I've been trying," I smirked playfully, but he just looked confused and went to get the chess set, which he then set up in the bed I'd slept in, while I gazed wistfully at him.

Keleon knew the rules of chess, but hadn't had much practice, so I beat him for the first four games. We mainly talked about chess and tactics, as well as other games we'd played. I flirted a couple of times, but as always, he didn't react. He won the fifth game, and I wasn't sure whether he was getting better or whether my concentration was waning. At any rate, I needed more food.

"That was fun, but I'm going to take a snack break," I told him, standing up.

"Worried I'll beat you now that I'm winning?" he teased, as he started to pack the pieces away.

I snorted.

"You've won one game out of five, it's hardly a winning streak. I'm just hungry."

He laughed softly, and it was so endearing, my heart nearly exploded. My feelings for this guy were only growing, and I desperately wanted to know how he felt about me. I couldn't remember a time I'd ever had a crush on someone this badly.

I dragged myself away from him to get a food pack and peeled the foil off. This one smelled like it might be imitating dried fruit of some kind. It turned out to be slightly chewy and kind of sweet, which confirmed my suspicions. I got through three packs of different food types, which didn't exactly go together. But since there was nothing to tell me what was in each one, I didn't get a lot of choice. I downed a whole bottle of water alongside my snacks.

While I was eating, I decided that I needed to try to kiss Keleon. Today. He was impassive to my unsubtle hints, and I had no way of interpreting what that meant, other than I wasn't being rejected.

There was now about twenty-four hours until we reached Epsilon 4, and I might never see him again after that. Actions spoke louder than words, and there would be no way he could ignore me kissing him. Even if it meant awkward silences for the rest of our trip, I had to know one way or the other because this state of limbo was worse.

Chapter 4 - The Kiss

I tidied up my mess and slipped into the bathroom to get another chewable teeth-cleaning tablet, before I went back to the bedroom, where Keleon was sitting upright on the bed with his eyes closed. I couldn't even see him breathing, he was such a perfect statue.

"Am I interrupting?" I asked.

His eyes opened and looked at me, otherwise unmoving.

"Meditating," he said.

"Oh, I'll leave you to it," I said, wishing I hadn't said anything.

"I was finishing anyway," he said, his dimple appearing as a smile filled his features.

"So, you meditate a lot?" I asked, genuinely interested.

"As much as I can," he responded. "My family believe that we're guided by a higher purpose, and meditation helps us to find our path."

"Wow," I breathed, genuinely taken aback. "I didn't realise you were so spiritual."

He laughed his gentle laugh, swelling my heart.

"There are no spirits involved, Damon. Our guidance comes from within. We just need to make sure we're listening."

"To yourself?" I asked.

That seemed a bit deep.

"I guess you would probably call it something like, 'following your instincts,'" he clarified. "And I'm trying to ensure my 'instincts' are finely tuned."

"You're pretty amazing," I gushed.

I was finding him more attractive with every passing minute. He was weird as fuck, but somehow that made him even more intriguing.

"Thanks," he said, barely acknowledging the emotion in my voice. "Do you have any interest in me showing you a bit more about flying the ship?"

"Seriously?" I asked, jolting back to reality. I was excited at the idea of understanding more about flying, but also about who would be teaching me. "Yeah, I'd love that. Did your instincts tell you that?"

He laughed, which was adorable, and shrugged.

"I don't know."

I followed him to the cockpit where we took our usual seats.

"So, I'll run you through what everything does, and then we'll take it off autopilot and you can try?"

"Great, yeah."

"Right. But no thrusters, seriously, we can't have anyone following us."

"Understood, captain," I grinned at him.

He set about explaining the basics about what things did and how they worked. I listened intently to my favourite guy talking about my favourite subject. It didn't get much better than this.

Every now and again, when Keleon pointed to one of the displays, or when he explained how a lever worked, our hands would brush against each other. I'd feel the sensation travel through my whole body, but mainly as a tightening in my chest or a shiver up my spine. The feeling of him touching my hand would stay with me, even after his hand had moved on to other things. I didn't want to wash my hands ever again.

God, the way I felt about him was so crazy.

After a couple of hours, he let me loose flying. I couldn't do much because he didn't want to arouse suspicion, but I didn't know too much more than the basics anyway. It was nice to feel in control of the vehicle though. After I'd had my fill, I handed the controls back to Keleon.

"That was awesome," I told him sincerely.

"I'm glad you liked it," he grinned.

He talked me through the settings, as he reset the course and went to put the autopilot back on, pointing to one of the larger control devices as he did so.

"I've learned that this one's a bit stiff, so it needs a bit more push than it normally should," he said, pushing the device extra hard. "I suspect it's because one of the components under the panel needs lubricating, but there's no point looking until we're docked."

I tried to take remove my mind from the gutter, but it was hopeless when Keleon was looking so damn sexy all the time.

"Something somewhere definitely needs lubricating. Especially if you're going to talk to me about things that are stiff, and any pushing related to them."

I raised an eyebrow playfully.

But, as usual, he just looked at me blankly. Like he was confused.

"I really enjoyed playing chess with you before. If you're still not hungry, do you fancy another game?"

"Sure," I blinked, nodding.

How could someone who was so in touch with his inner spirit, or whatever it was, be so oblivious to my intentions?

Soon we were sitting on the bed, with enough room between us for a chess board. I watched him set up the game, and I suggested that I should be black this time, so that he would 'make the first move.'

He still didn't see the irony.

I don't know whether Keleon beat me because I was somewhat distracted by my self-imposed mission for the afternoon, or whether he was genuinely improving. All I know is that as he was setting up the next game, I felt braver and more determined than I'd felt since we boarded this craft together. My pulse started racing as I realised there would be no better time to make a move than right now.

My heart was hammering in my chest as I shifted forwards, reaching across the chess board and putting one of my hands on each of Keleon's cheeks. He immediately looked up into my eyes, and his confusion was evident. I moved even closer, studying every inch of his beautiful face, not caring that the chess pieces were being knocked over and I was half-sitting on the chess board.

"What are you doing?" Keleon whispered, but he didn't try to resist.

"Following my instincts," I replied.

I moved my head forwards and gently pressed my lips against his. He tasted sweet, like cherries, and his mouth was soft and warm, and felt much better than I ever imagined it could. Keleon was motionless, not rejecting my advances. I moved my mouth slightly against his, and the sensation travelled all the way through my body. He appeared to be letting me do this, so I continued to plant soft kisses on his lips for the next minute or so, until, to my delight, he started to move his mouth in sync with mine.

The sensations left throughout my body by the kisses were getting stronger, and the hammering of my heart hadn't slowed down. Kissing Keleon was incredible. I didn't want to stop, but I figured we now had stuff we should probably work out. And if talking didn't go in my favour, at least I had this sensational memory to treasure.

Reluctantly, I pulled back and took my hands away from his face, trembling slightly with nerves, but smiling.

"So, does this mean you're into guys?" I asked him.

Keleon smiled back at me.

"Into guys? I don't understand."

Did I really have to spell this out?

"It means I'm gay and I'm trying to figure out your sexuality, so I know whether pursuing you is a good idea."

That was about as blunt as I could be. There was nothing ambiguous there, and yet I was met with silence from Keleon.

Awkward.

"So, you know, do you like men?" I prompted again.

"Gender doesn't make any difference to me," he replied softly, gazing into my eyes in a very distracting way.

"You're pansexual?" I tried to clarify if that's what he was getting at.

"If that means I don't distinguish between genders, then I guess so?" he offered.

"You don't know your sexuality?" I asked.

He looked blank.

OK, so maybe he didn't. I ran my fingers through my hair. Maybe I needed a different approach.

"OK. So ... it seemed like you liked me kissing you. At least, you didn't seem to object?"

He reached out and touched my lips with his fingers. It did all sorts of things to my body that made me want to get even more physical him, but I kept still while he explored my bottom lip.

"You mean when we touched lips?"

I nodded, trying to focus on the conversation rather than my urge to jump him.

"You've not been kissed before?"

"No, but I liked it. Why did you do it? Was there some reason?" he asked, and I couldn't help but feel this was all getting really fucking weird.

"It means that I like you." That was an understatement, so I rephrased. "It means I like you a lot."

"I like you too Damon," he confirmed, and my heart did a little jump for joy. "I didn't know affection could feel this ... nice."

Apparently, he liked me kissing him, and I thought I would burst with excitement.

"Nice enough to do it again?"

I was aware that I was staring at his lips and moving my face closer to his.

Keleon nodded his consent.

I kissed him with the same small kisses on his mouth that I had previously, savouring every second. Between kisses, I shuffled the rest of my body forward, so I was sitting partly on his side of the chess board and almost in his lap, my legs resting on top of his. Only then did I sneak my tongue across his mouth, and he hummed his approval. His hum went straight to my groin and I inadvertently let out a small noise of my own.

After that, my tongue crept across his mouth again and again, until he took the hint and parted his lips, letting me explore deeper. My hands pushed through his hair and I fisted the back of his head as the sensations got more intense. I groaned with pleasure and pushed him backwards, so that he was lying on the bed with me on top. His tongue ventured into my mouth for the first time, and, oh God, it made my body feel like it was soaring. As he kissed me back, I went higher and higher, well on my way to heaven.

Fuck, this was amazing.

Then Keleon broke the kiss unexpectedly.

"Um, Damon?" he asked, his tone suddenly serious.

"Yeah?" I breathed, trying to gain some control, but still feeling like I was floating.

Keleon's eyes darted around the room, which prompted mine to do the same. All around us, objects were floating in the air, including the green towel I'd used earlier, and the box of chewable teeth-cleaning tablets. A white bishop from the chess board caught my eye as it drifted past. I looked at Keleon, and behind him I saw the pillow and blanket from the bed floating under him. Which meant we were...

Falling. Everything that had been floating landed with a thud at the same time, including us.

"What the hell was that about?" I exclaimed as I rolled off Keleon and sat up.

"I have absolutely no idea," was his response. "I'm going to check the artificial gravity settings."

He swung his legs off the bed and disappeared, leaving me alone on the bed with my lips still tingling. As I lay there, eyes closed and touching my lips with my fingers, I tried to recapture every moment of what just happened so I could keep it in my memory forever. Grinning to myself, I pulled the pillow into an embrace, and concluded that kissing Keleon was the best idea I'd had in a long time.

Chapter 5 - The Arrival

I was still on cloud nine a full ten minutes later, when I finally stopped grinning insanely. I packed the chess board and pieces back into their box, since they were still strewn over the bed and the floor. Still smiling, I made my way into the cockpit of the small spacecraft to join Keleon.

He was just climbing out of a hole in the floor, his toned arms showing off his tight muscles either side of his armless T-shirt as they lifted his weight out of the cavity. I wanted to press rewind and watch him do that again.

"I couldn't find anything wrong with the artificial gravity," he said thoughtfully, as he looked up at me with those crystal blue eyes, wiping his hands on a cloth.

"Do you think it could have just been a glitch that rectified itself?" I asked.

"I thought that too," he replied. "So, I checked the system. According to the logs, there was no glitch. As far as the computer's concerned, the gravity was fine."

"Maybe the computer got it wrong?" I offered. I hadn't had much experience with computers, so I didn't really know if this was possible.

"I've never known a computer to not log a technical glitch," he said. "However, I guess it could be possible, theoretically." He shrugged. "Well, we saw things floating, and it seems like the only explanation left. Still, it's probably a good idea to check the other systems in case we have a bigger problem."

Keleon got to work, checking various other systems. He talked me through what he was doing and how he was doing it, and I felt like I learned quite a lot from him. I asked lots of questions, but I didn't feel like I helped that much, other than pass him tools now and again. Best of all, I got to see yet another side of him; a side that had a great depth of knowledge about ships' systems. I remembered he also had a great deal of knowledge about nuclear reactions in different star types as well as being a good pilot. He was certainly intelligent.

After we finished the system checks, I grabbed some food and water from the ration store and sat in the co-pilot chair next to Keleon, who was back in the pilot's chair.

"Hey," I started. "Can I ask you something?"

"Sure," replied Keleon, facing me with his feet still up on the dashboard.

"So, you're pretty amazing. You know all sorts of things about stars and planets. You can fly a ship, fix a ship and break someone out of a medical facility ... but you seriously didn't recognise I was flirting with you?"

"I don't know what 'flirting' is," he admitted.

"Oh, OK," I uttered, although I probably shouldn't have been surprised, given the way he'd been acting. I wasn't sure how to describe it though. "Um, flirting is when one person is saying suggestive things to another person, or acting a certain way, hoping that it may result in something like kissing."

"And you were doing this with me?" he asked, looking slightly confused.

"Yeah," I admitted, slightly sheepishly. "I guess you haven't had many people flirt with you?"

Although with him looking that gorgeous, I couldn't imagine why not.

"I've spent a lot of time on my own," he said. "I like exploring. Being out in space. I don't often have a lot to do with others."

"Right, makes sense."

And it did. If he wasn't around other people much, he wouldn't have experienced innuendo and flirty banter before. I hadn't too much myself, being essentially behind a forcefield for three years, but there were other people there, and some of them did a little flirting. And of course, there were films.

"We're scheduled to arrive at Epsilon 4 tomorrow morning, right?" I confirmed with him.

"Correct, we should arrive tomorrow morning, Selenia time," he replied. "Although it's likely to be afternoon on our location on Epsilon 4."

It was now evening, and we'd soon need to sleep.

"It seems we don't have that much time left alone together," I pointed out. "A substantial amount of which will probably be spent sleeping," I added, letting my eyes wander over his body.

"Correct," said Keleon.

"Any suggestions for what we could do with the remaining time?" I blinked at him innocently.

Realisation flickered across his features.

"Are you ... flirting?" he asked.

"There might just be hope for you yet," I smiled. "But in the meantime, I'm happy to make things easier for you. Would you like to join me in the bedroom?"

I offered my hand and he took it.

"Do you want to kiss me again?" he asked as he followed me, fingers threaded through mine.

"I certainly do," I replied, leading him to the bed, where I sat down and guided him to sit down with me. I wrapped my arms round his neck and savoured his crystal blue eyes, the way his dark hair flopped over his forehead and his dimples when he smiled back at me.

"Do you know how attractive you are to me?" I breathed, as I absentmindedly played with a piece of hair at the back of his head.

He cocked his head slightly.

"I guess sometimes it works that way. But nobody's had this reaction to me before."

Part of me wanted to ask what the hell he was talking about. But I was getting kind of used to him saying weird things, and the desire to feel his cherry-flavoured lips connected with mine again won that battle.

We spent the rest of the evening making out, moving tenderly and slowly, with tongues in each other's mouths and hands in each other's hair, until I was so tired, I couldn't stay awake any longer.

****

The next morning came at me in the form of the floor colliding with my face. I could only assume that my body was still adjusting from being used to having more space to sleep in, and I'd fallen out of the tiny fold-out bed.

I guess waking up in Keleon's muscular arms was a little too much to ask from the universe.

After freshening up and helping myself to some rations, I went into the cockpit where Keleon was watching the stars. My heart flipped the second I saw him.

"Morning, gorgeous," I said, walking towards him.

He looked round and smiled at me.

"Hi," he replied. And then, after a brief pause, "Are you flirting again?"

I turned him back round to look at the stars. And then leaned over, wrapping my arms round his shoulders from behind his chair.

"I was just letting you know I find you attractive," I beamed.

I wasn't sure if I could ever stop touching him in some way, now that I knew he was unlikely to object.

"I know, you told me that yesterday," he stated.

I laughed. That response was so typical of Keleon. Now I knew that it wasn't a negative response, it was easier to be relaxed about it. I was finding I really liked his quirky nature.

"I didn't think it would hurt to remind you," I said. "Besides, I like telling you." I kissed his cheek and let my face rest against his. "What are you looking at?"

He pointed ahead and slightly left.

"Tetra Prime," he said. "It's the second star to the left of that cluster, the bright one."

"You like Tetra Prime?" I asked, our cheeks still pressed together as we looked out to his star.

"The fifth planet of that system supports life," he said. "The life is very primitive, just animal and plant life, but it's really very beautiful. The climate is temperate. Mia and I spent a few days there once. I guess you might have called it a holiday. We hand-fed some of the wildlife and explored the mountains and waterfalls. It was nice."

"Sounds lovely. Why would you ever leave?" I asked.

"Well, I guess Mia and I are both explorers at heart. We never really stay in one place for long. We like to see different things, have different experiences."

It made sense. I knew what it was like to be in the same place for three years. Even if it were the most beautiful place in the universe, if it was all you ever saw, it might get a bit stale.

"Hmmm," I agreed. "Who's Mia?"

I realised I hadn't heard him talk about anyone else before.

"She's my travelling companion and my friend," he said. "She'll be waiting for us when we dock. You'll like her."

I hoped I would get along with Mia. I wondered whether she was quirky like Keleon. I couldn't work out what Keleon's friendship circles would be like.

"I'm looking forward to meeting her, then," I said genuinely, and he smiled.

"I need to start manual flight," said Keleon. "The autopilot only follows specific routes. I need to land manually and we're getting close."

"Sure," I said pecking his cheek and unwrapping my arms from his shoulders, pulling back.

"You don't have to move," said Keleon. "Unless you want to."

My heart did a little flip. Was Keleon initiating intimacy? Taking the lead in our continued closeness? Maybe he wasn't just reacting to my advances anymore. It seemed like he was actively seeking physical affection. I knew it wasn't an actual request for engagement, but it was the closest to one I'd had from him.

"I just didn't want to distract you from concentrating on controlling the ship," I reassured him, wrapping my arms back round him over the back of the chair and pecking him on the cheek. "But I'm more than happy to stay put if you want me around."

"You'll have to buckle up as we enter the atmosphere," he said, and I took that as a Keleon way of saying, 'yes, I want you around until we enter the atmosphere.'

He switched off the autopilot and talked me through the decisions he was making. A lot of it was similar to the flight lesson I had before, but some aspects were new. I asked various questions that he seemed happy to answer. And all the way, I kept my arms round him, and pecked him on the cheek periodically.

We started getting closer to a planet is a system orbiting a yellow dwarf star. It was smaller than Earth, but similar colours; browns, greens and blues. As we got closer, it seemed the land masses mainly consisted of a broad archipelago, containing lots of little islands, scattered over the planet's surface, like the lego blocks that used to end up strewn across by bedroom when I was a child.

"That's Epsilon 4?" I surmised, as Keleon had only talked me through how to get to the system, and not where we were going when we got here.

"It is," he confirmed. "The atmosphere is similar to Earth, which it why it was chosen as our base. Now would be a good time to buckle up."

Reluctantly, I pulled myself from him and strapped myself into the co-pilot's seat. He also strapped in.

"I'm going to put the ship in orbit until I've spoken to Mia," he said. "We've had to keep long-distance radio silence, so she wasn't sure when I'd be back. We're within range of talking on the short-range communication system now. I know where to land but I need to know she's in the hanger so she can open the hatch."

Once we were successfully in orbit, Keleon tried to contact Mia a few times without success. When she did eventually pick up, she sounded excited.

"Keleon, you made it! And you have Damon?" came the female voice through the communicator.

"I have Damon," he replied. "Can we initiate the landing sequence?"

"Doing it now. You have the coordinates?"

"I do," he said, and talked me through how to land it as we started to come out of orbit and started a controlled descent.

The group of islands he'd pointed to became larger as we descended, and I started seeing more detail that looked like it may be colonies and vegetation. We descended into a large hanger, which was housing another two spacecraft.

"Ready?" smiled Keleon as we unbuckled and stood.

"I guess so," I replied.

As the docking clamps locked us in place, my stomach twisted with nerves.

I had no idea what I was walking into.

Chapter 6 - The Friend

Keleon pushed the button next to the door to release it, and it lifted for us to exit. He smiled again as we exited the craft and waved to a pretty lady, who was probably in her early twenties. The lady's dark ginger hair was loose and fell over her shoulders. Wearing a dark green T-shirt and brown leggings that looked like they had oil on them, she was walking towards the door of the craft.

"Mia," waved Keleon, and started moving towards her.

I followed, assuming that was what I was supposed to be doing.

"Keleon," she said, waving back.

As they reached each other, they hugged for a few seconds. When they parted, Mia stood back slightly and examined him, from head to toe, including inspecting round the back of him.

"Wow," she said, as she came back round to the front of him again, still looking up and down. "I'm loving your new look!"

"Thanks," he responded with that cute dimpled smile.

Her comment made me wonder what he normally wore for her to be inclined to make that remark. I decided maybe I didn't want to know. He looked hot in the vest top and jeans; I should just be happy with that.

Mia's gaze wandered over to where I was standing. No doubt I was looking slightly awkward.

"You must be Damon," she said, reaching out her hand, which I took and shook firmly.

She seemed to be aware, as I now was, that Keleon was unlikely to make the introductions.

"Yeah, I guess you're Mia then," I replied.

"I am. Nice to meet you Damon. There is so much we need to talk about, but first I want to make sure you're comfortable," she said, gesturing for us to follow her. "We've set up a makeshift camp from some of the old storage rooms in the hanger. Basically, it's just blankets on the floor and a space we have for food, but we're not planning to be here too much longer anyway. Let me show you."

As we were following Mia across the hanger, I saw a familiar face coming toward our little group. I couldn't quite place it at first, because it was so out of context, but the jolly smile was hard to mistake.

"Aunt Helen!" I almost squealed as I ran into the embrace of the jolly fifty-something sister of my mother. I must have been about thirteen the last time I saw her, and her hair had silvered somewhat since then. We stayed like that for a good minute or so, until I let go.

"I didn't know you were going to be here," I said.

Mia faced Keleon, but she was smiling.

"Keleon probably didn't see how it would be relevant."

Keleon shrugged.

"I fail to see what purpose it would have served. Damon was going to find out anyway."

My stomach did a little flip when he said my name. I liked hearing him say it a little bit too much.

I looked over and smiled at the quirky man who didn't understand why I might have wanted to know my aunt would be waiting for me.

"I think Mia was probably showing you where we're set up," said Helen. "So, I'm going to leave you to it for now. I have some things I need to do, so I'll catch up with you later. Ask Mia for some food too. It's so good to see you again Damon!" she finished enthusiastically, planting a big kiss on my cheek while she embraced me again. So typical of Helen.

"This way then," said Mia, leading us to a small door the East of the main hanger room. "Toilet, in case you need it," she said, opening the door slightly so we could see and then closing it again.

She then took us through a door to something that looked like a storage room. There was a pile of blankets piled neatly in the corner of the room that had various boxes and containers pushed up against walls. The window on the far wall had a screen that could be pulled across to block out the light from the sun if needed.

"We've put you in here, Damon, I hope that's OK. It means you have a bit of space to yourself if you want it, and somewhere to sleep." Mia gestured to the blankets. "It's pretty basic compared to what you're probably used to."

"It's perfect," I replied. "I'm just grateful to be out of there."

"I bet," she said. "Food is this way," she left the room and walked up a small corridor to another storage room.

As she opened the door, I saw boxes of the ration packs we had on the ship, but also boxes containing fresh produce. Mia nodded at the fresh food.

"These things grow on the island. We try to get some every day and top it up. I recommend these," she continued, holding up something thin and orange, around the size of a finger. "They're yummy!" She put it back in the box.

Mia was very likeable, and I felt comfortable around her already.

"I'll make sure I try one," I assured her.

"Please help yourself whenever you like. As for you," she said, turning to Keleon. "You probably want a room too. I reserved you one at the back so you can meditate with minimum noise if you need to."

We followed Mia back down the corridor, and off a little passageway to the side. The set-up in Keleon's room was similar to mine, with some blankets and storage boxes. They both went inside, while I hovered at the door.

"This OK for you?" she asked him.

He looked around.

"I've got everything I need, thank you Mia."

Then Keleon stepped closer to Mia. He put one of his hands on each of Mia's cheeks. He closed his eyes and kissed her lips tenderly, running his hands back so that they tangled in her hair. His mouth moved against hers gently, just like mine had against his when I first kissed him.

I couldn't believe what I was seeing. My stomach lurched and twisted so much that it felt like someone was trying to rip out my insides. The temperature seemed to increase a couple of degrees as fury started taking hold. I felt my bottom lip start to quiver and blinked back the tears that had started to form in my eyes.

I thought he'd said they were just friends?

Chapter 7 - The Special Person

I didn't want to see him kissing her anymore. I couldn't. It was hurting way too much. With tears stinging my eyes and blurring my vision, I stumbled to the food store. Shaking, I grabbed a few pieces of food and a bottle of water and disappeared into my allocated room. A low tremor rumbled through the hanger, which I assumed was a ship either taking off or landing. I closed the door and looked for a way to lock it, but there didn't appear to be one. I thought about moving one of the storage boxes in front of the door to block it, but I was feeling weak and shaky, like all my energy was being drained. I didn't want to see Keleon ... I needed to block the door.

But who was I kidding? It's not like he wanted to see me any more anyway. He was otherwise engaged. I collapsed on my pile of blankets, thinking I should really eat something, but I wasn't convinced my stomach would hold onto it. I blinked and felt my cheeks get wet, as anger turned to dejection and self-pity.

I was so stupid to think that someone as stunning as Keleon would only be exclusively interested in me. He could have anyone he wanted. Mia was pretty, and he was pansexual. It made sense.

I peeled open a ration pack and slowly forced the food down, with something that was green and fresh, and if I could have tasted it under normal circumstances, probably would have been sweet and enjoyable. But it was tainted with the bitterness of rejection, and after that I still had the task of forcing it past the lump in my throat. At least I was managing to keep it down. The tears hadn't stopped falling though. If anything, there were more and more of them. I had been right there watching. Surely, he must have been aware of that?

I chastised myself for letting myself get so wrapped up in someone I hardly knew.

I managed to finish the rest of the food and had just curled up on my blanket in a foetal position, when there was a soft knock on my door. I didn't answer.

The door opened a crack and Keleon poked his head round.

"Damon?" his soft voice reached out.

My body tensed, but I didn't change position.

I answered him with venom in my tone.

"What."

"You disappeared suddenly."

"No shit."

"Are you upset?"

"What the fuck do you think?"

"I think you're upset."

"I am upset, Keleon."

He entered the room fully and closed the door softly behind him.

"I don't understand why. Can I help? Do you want to talk about it?"

The anger started building again and I pulled one of the blankets over my head, growling loudly. There was another low-level rumble in the hanger, but I was too angry to process it properly. How could he not know what I was upset about?

I tried to compose myself and pulled my head out from under the blanket.

"You kissed Mia."

"Yes."

"Just 'yes'? That's it? Just 'yes'?"

I rubbed my hands through my hair in frustration.

"I'm not sure what else I should be saying."

I knew my tone was angry. I was nearly growling at him.

"Jesus Christ, Keleon. I thought ... I mean, it felt like we were a couple. I thought I was the one you were with."

He looked confused.

"So, once we've kissed each other, we're bonded for life?"

I couldn't work out whether this was sarcasm or naivety. If it were anyone else, I would have gone for the former, but this was Keleon, and I already felt like he didn't have too much experience with ... well, people in general.

Besides, he looked like he was genuinely waiting for an answer, and he had come to talk to me off his own back. His tone was curious, not angry. I ran my hands through my hair again.

"No, we're not bonded for life or anything. It's just ... I just ... you know, though what we had was special."

"I thought so too."

"So why did you go and kiss Mia?"

"Because I like her."

"Because you like her?" Jesus Christ. Jealousy gripped me all over again. "And what about me?"

"I still like you, Damon. I don't understand why you think I might not? I'd be happy to kiss you as well." His voice was full of frustration. "You were the one who told me that kissing was for people who like each other."

"For people who ... Oh, my God."

I closed my eyes and pinched the bridge of my nose to try to calm myself down. If this had been anyone else, I would have told them to go to hell. But I had this uneasy feeling that he genuinely believed every word he said. Literally.

I inhaled deeply and breathed it out slowly, trying to think this through.

"Sit down," I instructed, and he came and sat on the blankets near me, but not too close.

In my mind, I went over our conversation on our journey here, the one he had just referred to, where we were talking about me kissing him.

"Why did you do it? Was there some reason?"

"It means that I like you. It means I like you a lot."

I realised that he was right; I had told him that. I also recognised that he and Mia had been good friends for a long time, and as such, probably fell under the definition of 'liked each other a lot.' I took another deep breath.

"I did say that, didn't I? That I kissed you because I liked you a lot."

"You did," he agreed, nodding.

"OK, then I need to clarify what I meant," I said, slowly realising that the cause of the problem may that he may have taken me more literally than I had intended. I reminded myself that he had spent a lot of his adult life travelling, and he may not understand how relationships work. "Kissing is for people who like each other a lot. But it's not usual practice to kiss everyone you like. People often find one special person that they like more than all the rest. The kisses tend to be reserved just for that special person and not for anyone else."

"Oh," Keleon blinked. He looked like he was legitimately processing what I'd just said.

"Yeah, so, by kissing you, I was trying to tell you that I wanted you to be my special person," I continued. Calmer now, I moved closer to him. I took his hand in mine and held it gently. "By kissing me back, I thought maybe you wanted me to be your special person too. Then when you kissed Mia, I thought you no longer wanted me."

"OK," he said, almost child-like in his innocence. "So, does Mia now think I want her to be my special person?"

"I don't know," I admitted. "I've only just met her, and I don't know what she'll think. But you should probably choose which one of us you want to be kissing, so that nobody gets confused or hurt."

"In which case, I choose you," said Keleon, without any hesitation. "It feels right with you. I'm not sure exactly how to explain it."

Relief flooded through me. There was certainty in his tone about the decision he'd just made. The conviction in his voice was enough proof that he really had just interpreted my previous words in a very precise manner, and this was all a huge misunderstanding.

Reassured, I dried my eyes with the bottom of my T-shirt.

"It sounds like we both got confused," I offered. "I'm sorry for being angry with you. I just didn't understand why you were kissing Mia, and it upset me." I sighed. "Maybe this is my fault. You told me you hadn't been kissed before, so I should have realised there are other things that come with kissing that you might not know. People also normally formalise that kind of relationship with words. So," I took a breath and steadied myself, "I'm sorry for not doing this earlier, I should have made it clearer that I wanted you to be my boyfriend."

He cocked his head slightly and raised an eyebrow.

"Boyfriend?"

This was Keleon. Of course he didn't know what a boyfriend was.

"The special person."

"I see."

"So, I'm sorry for not making it very clear before. Let me try to rectify that now." I shuffled even closer over the blankets and turned his hand over in mine. "I'd like to ask you to be my boyfriend. Only if you want to, of course. However, before you answer, I want to be clear, that means that we'd only kiss each other and nobody else. It would be for as long as we both wanted. When one of us doesn't want that arrangement anymore, we'd just tell the other one, and then we wouldn't be boyfriends anymore, and there would be no more kissing each other."

I hoped that was clear enough for him.

"OK, I understand," he nodded. "That sounds like something I want. But this is all new to me, so there may be other things that I don't understand. What happens then?"

"Then we work it out." I gave him a smile to let him know it was OK. "That's part of being boyfriends."

I closed the small remaining distance between us and hugged him. It felt like we both needed it.

"I didn't like seeing you upset," Keleon murmured against my neck as his arms reciprocated my embrace. "Or knowing that I did something to trigger it. I really didn't know it would hurt you like that."

"I know, it's OK," I planted a small kiss on his neck as I spoke into it. "Everything you did was with good intentions. You can't be expected to know this stuff if you've never come across it before. I shouldn't have expected you to just know. I'm sorry."

We stayed in that position, with our arms wrapped round each other, for over a minute. It felt nice to be this close to him. Guilt crept over me, as I realised how confused he must have been. I really shouldn't have assumed we were starting a relationship, just because we'd been getting intimate. I was kicking myself for not talking to him about it earlier.

We parted naturally and I pushed his dark hair away from his forehead, but it promptly sprung back to where it had been. I left my arms loosely around the back of his neck.

"You OK?" I asked as I pressed my forehead against his.

"Yeah," he whispered. "You?"

"Yeah," I answered truthfully. "I am now." I thought about what triggered this entire event. "But we should be aware there's someone else that might not be."

"You're right," he acknowledged. "I need to talk to Mia, don't I?"

"It's probably a good idea." I agreed. "I can come with you if you like. Or if you'd rather go alone, that's fine too. Your choice Keleon, I'll do whatever will help you the most."

His ocean-blue eyes looked pensively into mine for a few seconds. "I'd like you to come with me," he decided.

"Then I'll come with you," I smiled at him, releasing his neck and standing up. I held out my hand. "Let's go talk to Mia."

Chapter 8 - The Rules

K eleon knocked softly on the door to Mia's storage room.

"Come in," she called in a cheerful voice.

I felt a knot in my stomach as we entered. I'd only met Mia today, and had no idea how she'd react to any of this. I wondered how Keleon was feeling. I gently squeezed his hand in encouragement, which I'd been holding since he took it when I offered it to him. We had to do this; it wasn't fair to Mia otherwise.

Keleon opened the door and entered first, I followed him and closed it behind me with my free hand. Mia looked like she was sorting various tools into boxes, but she stopped and turned to face us with a smile.

"Can I talk to you?" Keleon asked Mia.

"Of course, Keleon. What's on your mind?"

As she spoke, her gaze drifted to out interlocked hands and she raised one of her eyebrows a fraction.

"I think I owe you an apology," Keleon started.

Mia lifted her index finger in the air.

"Stop," she commanded. "Let me guess. Damon kissed you but you didn't fully understand the context. You then kissed me, because you were left with the message that that would be an appropriate way of displaying your affection for me too. Now you've found out it's not appropriate, and you're about to apologise in case I've taken it the wrong way." She paused. "How close am I?"

She was smiling broadly and looking between Keleon and me.

"I would call that pretty accurate," I confirmed, raising an eyebrow of my own.

"How did you know?" asked Keleon.

"Oh, sweetheart, how long have we known each other?" Mia laughed softly. "I love you to pieces, but I'm in the least bit interested in pursuing anything romantic with you. And I know you don't feel like that about me, or it would have happened before now. Besides, I know you. I know how you might interpret experiences that are new for you and that you may take certain things out of context until it's explained." She paused again. "Also, there are other clues. Like, you've never shown any interest in kissing anyone before, although I appreciate we don't get many opportunities when we're travelling." She nodded towards our hands. "But then you walk in holding hands with Damon? Now it's clear where your sudden compulsion to kiss has come from."

"Why didn't you say something when I kissed you?" asked Keleon curiously.

"Because I didn't feel like it was my place." She took his free hand in hers. "This is one of those things I believe you kind of have to work out on your own, along with the person you've chosen to be with. You guys have to define your relationship, not me." She stopped and looked at me. "I have to say, though, it seems you're a good teacher Damon. It was actually a hell of a kiss. I'm impressed."

I felt my cheeks heat up.

"Thanks," I said, laughing.

Mia was actually pretty cool.

"So Keleon," she said, turning back to him. "I assume this means you have a boyfriend now."

"Yeah, it does," he replied, and he sneaked a dimpled smile in my direction. I felt a little giddy hearing him talk about me as his boyfriend to his close friend. Somehow it made it more real. This beautiful, quirky man was confirming out loud that he was mine.

"Then I should congratulate you," she said, beaming at him, "on your new adventure." She kissed him on the cheek. "And you, for taking him on," she winked at me and came to kiss me on the cheek too.

"I like a challenge," I replied, grinning.

I looked over to Keleon, but he was frowning, and I wasn't sure whether our playful banter had upset him. I squeezed his hand.

"You OK?" I asked, my smile fading as my boyfriend looked at me with a confused expression. Then he looked at Mia.

"You kissed both of us," he stated. His eyes narrowed slightly as he studied us for a few seconds. "And nobody seems to be upset this time."

I couldn't help but find it endearing that he needed this clarified.

"A kiss on the cheek like that is fine," I explained, touching my lips. "It's kissing on the lips that's only for your special person."

There was a pause while he looked between us again.

"Why are there so many rules?" Keleon pouted slightly, seemingly frustrated. "I like the kissing bit, but the rules seem overly complicated."

Mia and I laughed, and his face softened.

"You'll get the hang of it," she replied. He didn't look convinced. "You will, I promise," she assured him. "Listen, the sun will be setting soon. If you take a walk north of the hanger, you'll be near the water which is a great place to see the sunset. If you're interested, that is. I have to finish sorting the maintenance equipment, so I'll see you tomorrow, OK?" Then she winked at me.

Getting the hint, I turned to Keleon.

"Do you fancy a walk?" I asked him. "I'm still on Selenia time, so I'm not that tired yet."

"Yeah, that sounds really nice," said Keleon, as I opened the door to leave. "See you tomorrow, Mia."

We closed the door behind us and made our way to the main part of the hanger.

Chapter 9 - The Sunset

"I think north is probably that way," I pointed from close to where we landed the ship earlier.

"It is," replied Keleon. "I'm assuming you were paying attention when we landed then?"

"Of course," I grinned, and we headed out of the northwest hanger door and stepped into the evening air.

The atmosphere was serene, everything was calm and still. There was a slight breeze carrying the faint scent of the green fruit I remembered eating while in my room. Some of the thin orange fruits that Mia had suggested trying were also scattered around, and looked like lanterns hanging from their bushes. There was a worn track through the vegetation heading north, wide enough to walk side by side, so I pointed and suggested we followed it.

The air was still fairly warm, like a summer evening on Earth. I looked at the man I was holding hands with.

"This is nice already, and we haven't even reached any water yet," I observed.

"Yeah, it's so quiet," he replied. "I like it. And I like that I'm with you."

Heat filled my cheeks and happiness filled my heart.

"I like being with you too, Keleon," I said.

"I hope so," he said. "I feel like sometimes I just about get the hang of certain things, and then it turns out there's more I didn't know."

"Is there anything in particular that you want to know now?" I asked.

"Actually, there was something I wasn't sure of. Can we kiss whenever we like? Or are there some rules for that too?"

"It's a good question," I replied, as I stepped over a piece of debris on my side of the path. "It may make other people feel slightly uncomfortable if we kiss each other on the lips while we're around them, so when we're alone is probably better. But when we're alone, I can't imagine any reason I would object."

"OK, then, I'm glad I asked." He sighed. "Playing chess is logical. There's a set of rules and they don't change. But relationships? How do you even know what the rules are?"

"You learn from experience, I guess. Much like anything else. If you haven't had much experience, then you're not going to know."

"So, you've had lots of experience? Lots of boyfriends?"

"Actually, no, not really," I replied. "I mean, I fooled around a little bit when I was at school, but then at fifteen I was taken to that facility you got me out of, and there wasn't anyone there that interested me until you walked through the door. I guess I've learned a lot from films and talking to people at the facility about their experiences. Observations, mainly. I guess I've also seen the interactions between the parents of my friends."

"Not your own parents?"

"I've never met my father," I admitted. "My Mum told me that he disappeared from our lives before I was born. She also told me not to bother trying to find him as I'd never find him. It's not like I'd know where to start, anyway. My father's name is 'unknown' on my birth certificate."

"That must be tough."

"Well, not really actually. Mum's great, you know? And it's not like I've known life any other way. It's just been me and Mum. Talking of which, I should really send her a message letting her know I'm OK."

"I think Helen said your Mum would know that we have custody of you," he replied. "I think she's going to talk to you about it tomorrow."

Knowing that helped me feel better about not contacting her earlier. Keleon had been so ... distracting.

"OK, I'll make sure I talk to Helen tomorrow then," I said.

The path we were on opened up onto the shore of the sea. The waves were shallow and lapping against the ground gently. The sun was still in the sky, but slowly on its way to the horizon. Now that there was no vegetation, we could see two moons, on large and one small, and both turned pink in the evening glow of the sun. In addition, there was a thin faint ring that looked like it wrapped round the planet like one of Saturn's. In the distance I could make out the silhouette of one of the other islands.

"This is enchanting," Keleon said happily.

"Romantic," I added.

I would definitely have to thank Mia.

We found a place to sit next to each other, where the ground was springy, like we were sitting on moss. I leaned back on the palms of my hands with my legs outstretched as I soaked up the amazing view.

"So, what about your family?" I asked. "Do you get to see them much?"

"I'm very different to the rest of my family," replied Keleon, taking up a similar posture to me. "They think I'm strange and we don't talk much anymore. Mia says I'm the black sheep. I see her as my family now."

"I like her a lot already," I affirmed, recognising that Mia seemed to have accepted Keleon's quirks more than his own family had. "How did you meet her?"

"In a casino on the planet Gokk," he replied nonchalantly.

"You're a gambler?" I asked, shocked.

Keleon didn't seem the type and I was slightly taken aback.

He shrugged.

"It's a good way to get what I need to exchange for parts for ships and fuel. I'm actually pretty good at it, and I generally don't take more than I think I need to get by. My instincts help me."

"You and your instincts," I teased. "So, Mia gambles too?"

"Actually, not really. She was working in the casino as a gaming clerk. She helped run the games, but part of her job was also to identify anyone who looked like they were cheating. One of her colleagues accused me of cheating at her table one night. Of course, nobody could prove it, so they had to let me go."

Keleon had piqued my curiosity.

"Were you cheating?"

"I guess it depends on your definition of cheating. As far as I was concerned, I was just being myself. But I know my instincts probably helped me win. They seem to make me good at distracting others, so it probably did give me an unfair advantage. I don't see it as cheating, but I can see why others might."

"I know how distracting you can be," I confirmed with a grin. "So how did you end up with Mia?"

"Well, I went back the following night," he continued. "I thought I looked different enough that she wouldn't recognise me, but she did. She took me to one side, and we talked for a while. She asked me if I could get her out of there. She could have reported me to the management, but she didn't, so I thought it seemed fair to take her with me. Besides, I liked her."

"You're a good person Keleon."

"Well, taking her with me worked out nicely. Our partnership works well because we both have very different skills. I've taught her how to fly different ships and fix them, and she's been teaching me more about what drives people, and about social interactions. I still have a lot to learn, but she's very intuitive that way. We make a good team, and so we just stayed together. Mia says, 'if it ain't broke, don't try to fix it.'"

I chuckled.

"Yeah, I've heard that saying before. I'm glad you found her."

"Me too," he nodded. "She's changed my life. I can't imagine her not being in it now."

The sun was very low in the sky now, almost dipping into the water to the West of the island we could see in the distance. The moons had become darker pink, and the planet's ring could be seen more prominently in the sky. The only sound was the water gently lapping rhythmically in front of us.

"So, now I can add gambling to your list of amazing talents," I smiled at him. "Is there anything you're not good at?"

I raised an eyebrow suggestively as my eyes wandered over his body, not really expecting him to understand.

"I've seen that look before," Keleon smiled back, mirroring my eyebrow movement, and I melted at the comprehension in that was apparent his tone. "I think I know what it means now."

I was aware that he had turned his body slightly and his face was getting closer to mine.

"Do you?" I whispered, trying not to get my hopes up, but he continued to advance slowly in my direction and my heart began picking up speed.

"Uh huh," he breathed back, and I closed my eyes as my head started to spin.

For one invigorating moment I felt Keleon's breath on my lips, right before his soft mouth touched them and I tasted cherries. Every part of my body was suddenly paying attention. His mouth started moving against mine, peppering me with sweet kisses, before I felt nothing again and he spoke.

"You've changed me, Damon. I don't know how to explain it in words. Something about me feels different now, and I know it's because of you."

My eyes opened a fraction and his face filled my vision. Part of me understood, because I felt that way too. But part of me found it hard to understand that he could possibly feel about me the way I felt about him.

"Me too," was all I could manage before my eyes closed again and I waited in hope for him to enchant me with his lips again.

The next kiss felt a bit firmer and carried more conviction. Evidently, he was getting a little more confident. I felt drunk – giddy on the feeling of

Keleon initiating this level of intimacy and excited about him being more assertive. I liked the idea of him taking the lead, so I started to recline to let him do whatever he wanted.

"You're pulling back?" he asked when our lips drifted apart.

"Just getting comfortable," I reassured him.

"So ... should I continue?" he murmured against my lips as he followed me towards the ground.

"Definitely," I confirmed, as I felt the springy moss behind my head, enabling me to relax.

And continue he did.

Fireworks went off inside every part of me as our kisses deepened and I felt his tongue against mine. My hand wandered into his hair, while one of his rested on my waist. My other hand started to explore what was under his T-shirt, and I wasn't disappointed with what I found. He copied my action, his hand creeping under my clothes. His skin against mine made electricity flow through every nerve ending. The hand that I had in his hair started clutching at it, as my breathing got shallower and the kissing got deeper.

Keleon's hand moved over my skin, higher up my body, and my hormones went wild. There was nothing slow and tender anymore. What was going on inside my briefs had the potential to be embarrassing. I couldn't help but press it against his leg anyway. In return, to my relief, he pushed himself against my leg, letting me know he was in a similar state. Which, of course, did nothing to help calm me down.

That was when he started moving away from me. His mouth was still on mine, but the rest of his body felt like it was drifting away. I groaned in frustration. I wanted him pushed up against me again.

"No, come back," I pleaded against his lips, trying to move my body to meet his.

But all I met was air.

"I'm not doing anything," he said, breaking our contact completely.

With our caressing interrupted, I opened my eyes, dropping a short distance to the floor in an undignified manner with Keleon partially landing on top of me.

"What the hell was that?" I grumbled.

Keleon looked thoughtful.

"I don't know," he replied. "I think the kissing might be causing gravitational fluctuations." He looked at me pointedly. "Is that normal?"

"Kissing causing people to float?" I asked incredulously. "No, that's utterly ludicrous. There must be another explanation."

"Well, it only seems to happen when we're kissing," he stated. "That's three times now."

"Twice," I corrected him.

"No, three times," he repeated. "The other time you may not have realised because you fell asleep. It was on our way here, the last evening we were in the ship together. We weren't floating very high and we landed gently enough that you didn't wake up. After I made sure you were comfortable, I went and checked the artificial gravity again, but there was nothing in the logs that suggested anything was wrong."

"Why didn't you tell me?" I probed.

"It didn't seem important," he replied. "I assumed that since it was happening on the ship, there was something wrong with the ship's settings. I figured I'd investigate once we'd docked. But out here there's no artificial gravity, and so now the only thing connecting all the events is what we were doing at the time." He paused while I recognised the logic in what he was saying. "I don't know how, Damon, but I think something happens when we're kissing that creates a gravitational anomaly."

I ran my hands through my hair and sat up before looking back at Keleon. Could it be possible? It did seem like it was the only connection between the events.

"Oh my God, Keleon," I replied, a tight know forming in my stomach at the potential implications. "What if you're right?"

Chapter 10 - The Lab Rat

The next morning, Keleon and I were making our way to see my aunt, Helen.

The remainder of the previous evening had primarily been spent trying to think of alternative reasons for our mysterious floating incidents. We'd finally conceded to the likelihood that we wouldn't get an explanation without further investigation. We'd retired to our rooms with the intention of reflecting on it another time.

We knocked on Helen's door and she let us know we could come in with some excitement in her voice. She immediately swooped in for another hug and a kiss on the cheek. I noticed Keleon observing our interaction with interest.

"I'm so sorry I didn't get a chance to catch up with you yesterday," she said. "There were some things I really needed to take care of."

"No problem," I replied. "Mia and Keleon have been doing a great job of making sure I'm OK."

I shot a smile in Keleon's direction, which he returned.

"We're living on basics at the moment," Helen said. "But you're welcome to anything we have. It's been so long since I've seen you," she continued. "I can't believe how much you've changed, Damon. You're a man now."

"Yeah, it's been way too long," I replied. "What is it you're doing out here, anyway?"

"Sit down," she offered, pointing to her set of blankets. "There are things you need to know."

Helen went rummaging around in one of the bags that were at the side of the small room and pulled out a piece of paper.

"About three years ago, your mother met up with me, under the guise of a coffee and a chat," she said, handing the piece of paper to me. "It was all very pleasant conversation on the surface, but when she slipped me this piece of paper and put her finger to her lips, I knew people were listening to our conversation and that I needed to not ask questions."

I opened the tatty folded paper and read it out loud.

"'They've got Damon on Selenia. Get him out,'" I read. "Wow, that's quite extreme. Mind you, Mum never did like hospitals."

"With good reason, Damon," said Helen. "The outpost on Selenia isn't a hospital, or any kind of medical facility. It's a genetics research facility run by a group called Genetics In Action, or G.I.A. Their main purpose is to further the capabilities of the human race through genetic augmentation. Therefore, if one of their scouts finds someone with certain genetic markers, they investigate further."

"What? Why?" I asked.

"Any number of reasons. Not all humanoid species are friendly, so perhaps there are those that think it would be to our advantage to weaponize advantageous genetic traits. Financial reward is also a powerful motivator. Some humans will pay healthy sums to become stronger or faster."

"And they're allowed to do this?" I asked incredulously.

"Well, 'allowed' is a hazy word. They operate under the pretext of a medical research facility, on the grounds that they're advancing the treatment of unusual medical conditions. But there are a lot of us who suspect that isn't their primary function. Legally, they shouldn't be detaining you unless it's on medical grounds and it's beneficial for you. We think we're now in a position to challenge them if they try again, but they are a powerful organisation and we needed you on the outside before we could do that."

"They told me I was there because I had a blood anomaly and it could affect my health," I said, with the slowly sinking feeling I'd been lied to.

"You do have a blood anomaly, but as far as we know, it isn't doing you any harm," explained Helen. "Your mother knew that if G.I.A. ever found out about your blood, they were likely to attempt to harvest it and research it. Which is why, as much as possible, she kept you out of hospitals."

"Why didn't she tell me?" I asked.

"The fewer people who knew about it, the better," replied Helen. "If you didn't know about it, then if they used any techniques in an attempt to extract the truth from you, you wouldn't be able to tell them anything."

"But you knew?"

"Well, I don't know specifically what it is they're after," she continued. "Your mother just warned me when you were born, that something like this may happen one day. She didn't give me any further information in case they got it out of me, and it put you in jeopardy. It seems she's the only one who really knows the full story. The fewer people that knew, the better."

"I was a lab rat," I whispered, as the truth sank in. "So, you can't tell me what's in my blood that makes it so different?" I asked.

"No," confirmed Helen.

I thought back to the previous night, and the other incidents we hadn't been able to explain.

"This could sound like a really random question, but could it be something that distorts gravity locally?" I figured I might as well ask the question. "I mean, is it possible that it could make things around me float?"

"Have you been experiencing gravity distortions then?" she asked back.

"Yeah, I think so," I replied. "We haven't been sure what's causing them."

Helen shook her head.

"I don't know," she admitted. "I wish I had answers for you. All I know is that whatever it is, was genetically passed to you by your father."

"Which is why he's disappeared," I said, putting the pieces together. "Because if G.I.A. knew where he was, they'd be after him too."

She nodded.

"That's why he left us before I was born, then?" I asked.

"I don't even know whether he knows you exist," said Helen. "Your mother may not have told him, in her efforts to try to protect everyone involved." She took a deep breath before continuing. "The reason I was busy yesterday is because I was trying to put something together after I received a message that G.I.A. have your mother."

"What? No!" I cried.

Keleon reached out and touched me gently, letting me know he was there, and I gave him a grateful look, before focusing back on my aunt.

"She knew I would try to get you out," Helen continued. "But she also knew that I had no way of telling her when or how, so she visited you like she normally would. The only form of communication that wasn't monitored between us was paper, like we used to use when we were kids, and that's difficult to send across the galaxy."

"What will they do to her?" I asked, slightly panicked.

"They're not complete monsters, Damon. They'll probably just detain her until they get you back. Which, by the way, isn't going to happen, but it won't stop them trying."

"But they're detaining her illegally," I insisted.

"She's also the only one with the evidence we need to be able to prove that detaining either of you has been done illegally," replied Helen. "We need her out too, before we can do anything. I know she'd rather they detained her than see you in there being tested to death. But anyway, we're going to try to get her out. The main advantage we had before, other than Keleon's aptitude for getting into the building, was the element of surprise," she continued. "We don't have that this time, because they've probably guessed that we're going to be trying to attempt something. So, we need another advantage."

"Do we have another advantage?" I asked.

"Not yet, but I'm hoping we can get hold of one," rationalised Helen. "Yesterday I located a disrupter module. There aren't many around that would have the right frequency, so I don't know how long it would be before we could locate another one. The module can knock out enough electrics, at the right frequency, for us to be able to get into the building undetected and look for your mother. With any luck, it will also create confusion as well; they're be relying on their cameras and security equipment to locate us. If they're busy trying to get everything back online, it should distract them from what we're doing. Plus, it will disable any forcefield she's being kept behind."

"OK, great," I said. "How do we get this disrupter module?"

"Well, that's where it becomes trickier," she explained. "My sources tell me it's currently owned by a Kikorangi. Kikorangi generally don't like outsiders, so they're only likely to sell it to us if we're very persuasive."

She looked over at Keleon meaningfully.

"You need me to be persuasive?" he asked, smiling slightly, showing off his dimple again. "I'm up for retrieving it. What do you think they want for it?"

"We don't know," admitted Helen. "I didn't get that far. Have you got anything you think they might want?"

"I can have a look," replied Keleon, standing up, and moving towards the door.

"Thanks, Keleon," my aunt looked gratefully in his direction, and he nodded as he disappeared from the room. "Sorry to have dumped all that on you so suddenly," she said, focusing back on me. "Are you OK?"

"Yeah," I replied. It sounded like, at least for now, Mum was safe, even if it wasn't ideally where she wanted to be. And it sounded like we had some kind of beginnings of a plan going on to get her out. I was a little shaken, but not too bad. "Thanks for getting me out, Helen."

"I couldn't have done it on my own," she said. "Mia is the daughter of a very good friend of mine, someone I grew up with. She's young and vibrant and has the energy required to do the physical things I can't do any more.

As soon as she heard I was looking for help, she came straight here, and brought her travelling companion. Talking of which," she continued. "I saw the way you looked at each other."

I felt myself blush furiously.

"Yeah, we've established we like each other," I verified. "We're going to see where it takes us."

My aunt smiled widely.

"Aw, sweetheart, that's lovely," she beamed. "And I'm not trying to interfere, it's just that ... well ... with Keleon ... you're aware there may be some ... things ... he might not understand?"

"I'm aware," I confirmed confidently.

Everyone seemed aware that he'd not been in a relationship before and needed some help grasping some of the concepts. It was nice that people were looking out for him, and I had every intent of supporting him as much as I could.

"So, what's a Kikorangi?" I asked, shifting the spotlight away from my love life.

"Kikorangi is a word that means 'blue' in ancient Maori. We call their species that because of their blue coloured skin."

"Is their planet far away?" I asked.

"Not too far. It shouldn't take more than an hour or two to get there. We'll have to work out if we have anything of value to trade, and then our chief negotiator will probably need to meditate before he goes in."

"I'd like to go with him," I stated.

Partly because I wanted to see Keleon's negotiating skills, and partly because I just wanted to be close to him.

"I understand," she smiled at me. "We've only just got you back, and we need to make sure we don't put you in any unnecessary danger. Mia and Keleon possibly know more about the Kikorangi people, and whether it's likely to pose any kind of threat if you go along. So, let's consult them first and see what they think the risks are."

I continued to chat to my aunt about the facility I was being kept in, how Mum was, what life had been like for Helen since then and other things. It turned out Helen had spent a fair portion of the last couple of years trying to get together enough funding to buy ships and their parts, and of course assembling their little team. I was grateful for all the effort she'd gone to and wasn't sure how I could repay her kindness. She assured me that I couldn't, that her family was very important to her, and it was just nice to see me out of there at last.

About an hour later, the four of us were gathered back in Helen's room to discuss the disrupter module, and how we would get it. My stomach did a little excited flip as Keleon entered the room and smiled at me, and I wondered whether I would ever stop reacting to him like that.

"I've had a look at what I have available to trade with," he said to the group as he made himself comfortable on one of Helen's blankets. "It turns out I've got some fire opals. I believe the Kikorangi find them valuable because they don't naturally have any gemstones that colour on their planet." Keleon opened his hand to reveal a selection of the beautiful orange and red gemstones. "I could take those and some other gemstones with me to negotiate with."

"They're so pretty," I said, picking up a scarlet one and holding it to the light. The way the light refracted through it reminded me of a sunset.

"How do you feel about me coming with you?" I asked, as I gave Keleon back the precious mineral.

Keleon looked at Helen.

"Any objections?" he probed.

"I thought you'd probably be better placed to understand the risks than I am," she answered. "I haven't encountered the Kikorangi before, and you probably know more about them than I do. Obviously, we don't want to be putting Damon at unnecessary risk. But I also recognise that it may be just as dangerous for him staying here. What are your thoughts?"

"The Kikorangi aren't a violent people, but they're not keen on other races," replied Keleon. "They tolerate outsiders because their planet is beautiful, and the tourism brings them good business. If the outsiders don't bring anything of value, then they tend to just ignore them. They may not be very friendly, but they're not into attacking people either. It should be fine for Damon to come along. And besides, I'd enjoy the company."

He smiled at me, and my heart warmed at the idea that he wanted me with him.

"OK, so when's the best time to go?" I asked.

"The contact I've been given, Aryk, is willing to meet our representative whenever we're ready," Helen said. "The Pavo's been checked over and is ready to go. You could leave around lunchtime and be back before dinner, assuming all goes well. Keleon, does that give you long enough?"

Keleon pushed himself onto his feet.

"I'll meditate now, and check I have what I need," he said. "I'll meet you in the hanger at 13:00," he said directly to me, before leaving.

"I guess I don't need much," I said to the remaining ladies. After all, I was mainly going along to spend more time with Keleon.

My stomach chose that time to let everyone in the room know I was hungry.

"Sounds like you need food to me," teased Mia, and she stood up. "Come on," she nodded towards the door. "Let's grab something to eat before you go."

Chapter 11 - The Experiment

At 13:00, Mia and I approached Keleon in the hangar. He was standing next to the door of the Pavo, with one foot and his back resting on the entrance as he calibrated a small piece of equipment.

As soon as he caught my eye, I was mesmerised by his perfect features, and couldn't believe this Adonis was mine. I wondered whether there was any way to tell whether I was actually dreaming or not, because sometimes this still didn't feel real.

As my insides were turning gooey, Mia linked her arm through mine and put her mouth close to my ear. She must have noticed the way I was staring at Keleon.

"You're so whipped," she teased lightly, so that only I could hear her.

I turned to face her, slightly aggrieved that I'd been caught. But I softened when I saw her huge grin and mischievous eyes under her ginger curls.

"Yeah, I think I am," I reluctantly agreed, turning back to face the guy who was making me feel things I'd never felt before.

Keleon pushed himself away from the wall with the foot that had been resting against it, taking his eyes away from the device he was holding to look at us as we approached.

"Hey," he greeted as we reached the door.

I really wanted to kiss him, just a peck on the lips to return the acknowledgement, but I felt a little self-conscious with Mia there, so I put my hands in my pockets instead.

"Hey," I tried to sound casual.

"I've put some rations in the ship, along with some water, just in case we get delayed," Keleon informed us. "You never know what might come up."

"Cool," I said. "Did you get done everything you wanted to?"

"I did," he replied.

"OK, sounds like you guys are all set," said Mia. "Good luck Keleon, not that you'll need it. I'll do the docking clamps and hatch. See you this evening!"

I walked towards the door of the craft, looking behind me to wave at Mia as she danced away, ginger curls bobbing. She looked back and saw me looking at her, and grinning, mouthed the word "whipped" at me as she waved back. I rolled my eyes, but it wasn't like I could deny it.

I slipped into the co-pilot seat and started to buckle-up. Keleon followed me into the cockpit.

"You didn't want to take her out?" he asked.

I looked at him blankly, and he gestured towards the pilot's seat.

"You mean, me flying the ship?" I clarified.

"Yeah, you know enough to do this," Keleon replied. "And you're quick learner. I can talk you through the rest. Only if you want to."

"Oh my God, really?" I gasped. "Awesome!"

I unbuckled myself from the co-pilot seat and shifted over to the pilot's seat, while Keleon took the co-pilot seat, grinning.

Keleon talked me through the safety checks and what information Mia needed from us to release the docking clamps. When everyone was satisfied, I started the ship's ascent, under Keleon's detailed instruction. The island we had been docked on became smaller as we pulled away, and soon Epsilon 4 was melting away into the distance. Keleon showed me how to set the right course using the auto-pilot, and I could release control of the ship.

"That was amazing," I giggled, as I swung round in the pilot's chair to face Keleon. "I can't believe I did it!"

"You're a natural pilot," he said. "Do you want to land it as well?"

"Definitely!" I confirmed.

Flying a ship for an entire journey was such a great experience.

"I know you've read lot of books, but unless you put the theory into practice, it's sometimes hard to see how it all fits together," Keleon rationalised.

"Lots of things are like that," I replied. "Talking of which, don't we have a theory of our own that needs investigating?"

I couldn't help grinning. I was in a good mood after taking off successfully from Epsilon 4.

Keleon raised an eyebrow.

"You mean you want to investigate whether the gravitational abnormalities are linked to the kissing?" he asked, probably already knowing the answer.

"Maybe."

Or maybe I just wanted an excuse to kiss him.

"It will be about an hour before we need to start the landing process," he smiled, and the dimple was back. "We could investigate in the meantime."

We both unbuckled our straps and I leaned forward towards him, and he mirrored the action. I closed my eyes and as our lips touched, we gave each other a couple of chaste kisses. I pulled back and looked round.

"Nothing appears to be moving," Keleon observed.

We kissed again, lightly. But when we looked round, everything, including us, stayed put.

"You're right, it doesn't look like anything's happening," I remarked, surveying the cockpit for anything that looked like it was detached from where it should be. "Maybe this would be more comfortable on the bed. If we wanted to carry on, that is. You know, purely in the interest of science."

"In the interest of science, if we're doing an experiment properly, we should recreate the original conditions as much as possible," confirmed Keleon as he stood up.

I couldn't tell whether he was joking or not, but I didn't mind either way, as we made our way to the little pull-out bed where we had our first floating experience.

As we lay down together, I touched his perfect face, wrapped my arms round the back of his neck, and started to kiss him. After only a couple of minutes, curiosity got the better of both of us and we looked around, but nothing was happening.

Maybe Keleon had been wrong. Maybe something else was causing the gravitational anomalies and the timing was just coincidence.

Our mouths met again. This time I focused on how he felt when I touched him, how soft his cherry lips were and how his tongue felt when it met mine. Our legs intertwined, the kisses deepened, and it became easier to drift to a place where Keleon was everything. Our hands found each other's skin. My fingers started exploring just under the waistband of his jeans. My breath shortened, and my pants tightened as I thought about how close my hand was to unfastening his zip. Instead I forced my hand to curve round his waist and up his back to join my other hand.

Which is about the time that I realised that one of my arms should have been feeling the pressure of his weight, trapping it between him and the bed. I pulled back and looked down to where I thought the bed should be, and as soon as I did so, it came rushing up to meet us. We landed with a gentle bump, since we'd not been very high, and looked at each other. I propped myself up on one elbow.

"Looks like your theory was right," I sighed as the moment was lost.

Chapter 12 - The Kikorangi

"Do you think this is connected to whatever G.I.A. wanted with my blood?" I asked.

"It seems like the most logical conclusion, doesn't it?" replied Keleon.

"Yeah," I conceded. "How are we supposed to kiss each other now, without risk of injury?"

Keleon propped himself up too.

"That's what you're concerned about?" he asked. "We think there could be something in your blood that can create gravimetric distortions, and you're worried about how we should deal with the kissing?"

I felt like my priorities were reasonable, so I nodded and smirked a little.

"You're incorrigible," he responded, pushing me playfully, and I pecked him on the lips to prove where my priorities lay. "So, the kissing itself didn't seem to set it off. Nothing happened in the cockpit. So maybe it's not the actual kissing that's causing the distortions. Can you feel any kind of connection to it?"

"Um, not really," I confessed. "It's not like I knew what I was doing. I wasn't trying to get anything to float. I didn't even really believe it could have been me doing it until now. I haven't got the first idea how to connect to it or control it."

"OK," said Keleon, thoughtfully.

"I did notice that the floating didn't kick in until the kissing got ... intense. So maybe it's linked to my emotional state rather than the actual kissing?"

"It sounds like maybe it is," he agreed. "In which case we probably just need to be careful about your emotional state until we have a bit more time to figure it out."

"Shame," I pouted playfully. "I don't really want to be careful when I'm around you."

"Me neither," he said sincerely. "But it's just until things settle down, then we can take some time to investigate it more, OK?"

"Hmph." I kept pouting and pretended to sulk by crossing my arms and rolling over, but he rolled me back and pinned me to the bed.

"Damon?" he smirked at my antics. "We'll work it out, OK?"

I felt myself go weak at his promise to make things work with me, and I couldn't fake being grumpy anymore. He leaned down and kissed me gently, and then stood up.

"Until then, we have a ship to fly," he declared. "It's getting close to when we need to land, so if you want to land the ship, why don't I start talking you through what's going to happen?"

He took my hand and led us both back to the cockpit, with me in the pilot's seat and him in the co-pilot's seat. True to his word, he talked me through what was likely to happen as we entered the planet's atmosphere, and how we were going to land at the right coordinates by entering the orbit of the Kikorangi planet before adjusting course. Keleon reminded me that he had some of the controls on the co-pilot side and was able to take over some of the functionality if needed.

It wasn't long before we were approaching the blue planet, and I successfully took the ship onto the required flight path. We didn't need direction from a contact from the planet this time, because we planned to land in an open space, rather than in a hanger or docking bay. I lowered the craft gently towards the specified coordinates and was delighted when it ended up right where we'd agreed. Now I'd managed a full flight on my own (albeit under instruction), and I was proud of the achievement. I knew it has been a relatively simple journey, and I would need more training in order to do anything more complicated, but still, it was a good start. I smiled at my boyfriend who looked pleased with me too.

"Nicely done," he said genuinely.

"Thank you for the guidance," I replied. "You're a good teacher. You make everything simple and understandable."

It was true.

We stepped out of the craft and into the crisp air. The temperature was cooler than I was used to, but not unpleasant. The landscape was blue and white as far as I could see, with dips and rises like valleys and mountains, that glittered where the sunlight fell.

"Wow, this is pretty," I commented as I took it all in.

"This part of the planet is mainly composed of sodalite and white quartz," replied Keleon. "This is usually where the tourists and traders come, because of its beauty. The blue skin of the Kikorangi is thought to have evolved from a need for them to blend in with the sodalite for camouflage. The need for camouflage has now gone, of course."

We started walking towards the coordinates of the meeting point.

"I think the Kikorangi will like the fire opals I brought," Keleon continued. "They like gemstones with red and orange hues. As you can see, it's a rare colour around here." He gestured to the blue and white environment we were in. "I've heard they like fire opals, anyway."

"You know a lot about them," I noticed. "Have you been here before?"

"Not specifically," said Keleon. "I listen to stories people tell whenever I get the chance, so I can learn about different species. Isn't that part of being an explorer?"

"It is," I agreed. "So, the information you have ... you hear this stuff when you're gambling?"

"Well, sometimes," he nodded. "Or sometimes just talking to people that I meet in different places. I don't gamble all the time you know. I only take what I think I'll need to get by. Look," he continued in a softer voice, as we rounded a corner. "I believe this is the traders' area. This is where I'm supposed to meet Aryk."

In front of us opened up a large outdoor area, where there were a number of Kikorangi eating, drinking and talking. We were mainly obscured from their view by a large blue monument with a pointed tip. I looked back to Keleon, who was scanning the area.

"Do you have some kind of strategy?" I whispered.

I couldn't immediately see anyone that wasn't a Kikorangi and that worried me.

"Mia would call it 'winging it,' but relying on my instincts usually works for me," he replied.

"You don't have a plan?" I whispered incredulously.

It sounded like these Kikorangi weren't violent, but we could really do with that disrupter module, and leaving it to chance seemed a bit risky.

"Aryk said he would be wearing a green bracelet, so that I'd know who he was," he said thoughtfully, and blatantly ignoring my question. After a few seconds, he pointed and continued, "I think I see him. Next to where it looks like they're serving drinks."

I looked back towards the area and spotted a blue-skinned male with a green band around his left wrist. I studied the rest of the crowd. It looked like the males had no hair and the females had green hair, and I guessed that from this kind of distance, that was how you told them apart. I also looked harder and noted that there were no other species obviously in the area – it did look like it was purely an area for the Kikorangi.

"You'll need to stay here," said Keleon. "Try not to draw attention to yourself. The Kikorangi don't like outsiders."

I couldn't understand why Keleon thought he would fare any better than I would.

"So you keep saying," I started, as I turned back to face him. "You don't exactly blend ... Oh my God."

Standing beside me was a Kikorangi female, with long, grass-green hair, deep blue eyes and a shimmering aqua-blue outfit. Keleon was nowhere to be seen. I took a step back and, wide-eyed, looked her up and down.

I was about to ask her what she had done with Keleon, but then she outstretched her arm and examined it, turning it over so she could see the underside of it. She then looked down at the rest of her body.

"Interesting, I've never been blue before," she said in a feminine voice, looking up and beaming at me. "Wish me luck Damon."

"Keleon...?" I breathed.

'She' moved out from behind the monument, gracefully gliding over the courtyard of Kikorangi to where Aryk was sipping his drink, as I tried to process what was happening. My boyfriend currently looked like a female Kikorangi and I had no idea how. I concluded that the most likely explanation was that he must have some kind of holographic technology that I wasn't aware of. I'd have to ask him about it later because it was very realistic, and I wanted to have a go.

Aryk bowed low to Keleon when he saw 'her,' and 'she' returned the gesture. They talked for a while, exchanging bows every so often. I saw Keleon bring out a couple of the opals and pass them to Aryk, who held them between his fingers and looked at them against the sun. Aryk nodded, and shortly afterwards, it appeared that a bargain had been struck and an exchange had been made.

Keleon took the item and bowed to Aryk as 'she' departed, gently drifting back through the sea of blue towards me. I could see Aryk watching 'her' as 'she' disappeared from his view behind the monument to join me.

"One disrupter module," 'she' said, proudly displaying the piece of equipment in front of me. I glanced down at the module and then up to 'her' face. It looked so real. So authentic. The detail was incredible. I knew holograms could be quite lifelike, but I'd never seen a hologram this elaborate before. Perhaps technology had moved on while I'd been out of the picture for three years.

"Damon?" asked Keleon's feminine image, and then, as I watched, the shape morphed back into the version of Keleon that I was more familiar with. "You OK?" he asked, his voice back to the masculine version I was used to.

"Yeah," I managed, although it felt like it was a reflexive response rather than a reflection of my true feelings.

That transformation hadn't looked like a hologram.

Chapter 13 - The Vacillator

Keleon smiled and started walking back towards the space craft, and, on autopilot, I followed him.

Oblivious to my confused state, Keleon started telling me about the meeting with Aryk. He told me what the bowing meant, how Aryk seemed happy with the offer that was made and other details that I wasn't really paying too much attention to. The walk back to the craft felt surreal, like I was thinking too much, but at the same time I wasn't really thinking at all. I could hear the words Keleon was saying, but they sounded distant and flowed past me like a river, disappearing into the distance without me really hearing them. I couldn't tell whether the walk back to the craft was fast or slow, because time felt a little meaningless, like I was in a trance.

When we arrived in the cockpit, Keleon offered me the pilot's chair, but I shook my head and slipped into the co-pilot's seat. I couldn't focus properly, so there was no way I'd be able to concentrate on getting a space-craft out of the atmosphere.

I buckled up, and, as Keleon did the same and started the engine, the question that had been in the forefront of my mind, made its way to the front and out from my mouth.

"What was the holographic thing you did back there?"

"What holographic thing?"

"To give you blue skin. To make you look like one of them."

Keleon was acting like it was no big deal. He continued working on take-off like I'd asked nothing of consequence. I felt the craft rise into the air as he spoke.

"There was no technology involved, Damon." He pulled the controls and pushed the necessary buttons, while observing our surroundings with the monitor. "I'd forgotten you hadn't seen me shift before."

He smiled lightly in my direction before continuing with his navigation.

Keleon continued to make sure we were clear of the atmosphere and went about setting a course back to Epsilon 4.

Meanwhile, my body felt like a plethora of contradictions. I was too hot but had cold shivers running through every part of me. I sat rigidly but could still feel myself shaking. Time was moving too fast and too slow simultaneously. I felt like I was feeling every possible emotion at the same time as nothing at all.

All the time I was thinking. About all the strange things Keleon had ever said. About the way he needed explanations for things that I took for granted. About how it felt like we kept talking at cross-purposes when we first met. About the things he hadn't understood or taken literally along the way.

Oh God, I'd been so blind. What kind of childhood leads you to a place where you've never seen a kiss before? A childhood where you've never seen a film involving a kiss, or never seen your friends or your parents kiss?

I knew the truth before the words had finished forming on my tongue, and it turned my stomach.

"You're not human." It wasn't a question.

"Correct."

My stomach constricted so tightly that I felt compelled to double over to try to stop the pain. With my elbows on my knees, my palms pushed against my forehead as I tried to prevent the contents of my stomach emptying out. I felt my whole body trembling, and I wasn't sure whether it was coming from me or from the craft.

"Oh, God. You're not human," I repeated, processing the information more fully this time.

"We established that already," Keleon replied casually.

In that moment, my heart shattered into a million pieces. Confirmation that he wasn't what I had thought he was seeped through me. All those experiences we'd had together suddenly all felt fake. It was like I'd been punched in the gut. With hurt and anger battling for dominance, my vision became blurry. I blinked and felt my cheeks get wet.

A low rumble crept through the craft. A rumble that sounded like ... like the one I'd heard in the hanger on Epsilon 4 when I'd been angry before.

"Why the fuck didn't you tell me?" I asked, voice shaking as more tears escaped.

"You didn't ask."

"Didn't you think you should have mentioned it?"

"No, why would I have?"

"We've been kissing!"

The tears were still flowing along with the hurt and anger.

"Yes, because we like each other. And we both like kissing. What does that have to do with whether I'm human or not?"

Keleon finished making sure the autopilot was set and turned to face me, looking confused. Why did he not understand why I was upset? The anger was building.

"Because you ... you made me think I'd been kissing a human!"

The Pavo sounded like it was going to buckle under its own weight. Keleon looked around, concerned.

"Damon, I don't understand what's going on, but I think you may need to calm down before you rip the space craft apart," he responded gently. "I want to help you. I've never lied to you. I've never claimed to be human. Maybe you assumed I was. If I'd known it would be important to you, I would have told you, but it didn't occur to me that it would matter what species I was."

On some level I recognised that the Pavo may be reacting to my anger. No matter how annoyed I felt, it wasn't worth putting our lives in danger. I actively took a deep breath and counted to ten, as Keleon reached out and took my hand in his. I focused on his claim that he hadn't done this intentionally. I counted to ten a few more times, breathing deeply, calming down, but not enough to stop the tears falling. The craft sounded like it had stopped reacting to me, so I tried to form another question.

"So, if you're not human, what are you?" I managed to look up at him.

"Humans refer to our race as Vacillators because we can change how we look," he replied.

"So, you're a shapeshifter?"

"Correct."

"Jesus Christ!" I could feel my temper flaring again and the Pavo rumbled in response. "Do you even really look like this?" I gestured up and down his body.

"What a strange question," Keleon replied. "Of course I look like this."

"But you sometimes look like other things," I pointed out.

"Yes, and then I look like those other things. But right now, I look like this."

This conversation wasn't going the way I wanted it to. Maybe I worded my question badly. My mind was so confused that it was hard to tell.

"I meant, what do you look like when you're in your natural state?"

"I'm always in my natural state."

I ran my fingers through my hair and put my hand back in his. I needed answers. Which meant I needed to ask the right questions.

Deep breath. Count to ten.

What were the right questions?

"OK then. What do you look like when you're not pretending to be something else?"

"I never pretend to be something else, Damon. Humans also change how they look. Right now, you look like that." Keleon gestured towards my body as he spoke. "But you weren't born looking like that, were you? And when you get older, you'll probably look different as well. The way you look changes over time, but it's all still you. At each point in time, if you were asked, you would say you're in your natural state. Why would you think it would be any different for me?"

"Because I don't get to choose the way I look."

"Neither do I."

"But ... wait, what?"

"I don't choose my appearance. Nor do I choose when a change will happen."

"You're ... you're not choosing this?"

"No. It just happens."

"So ... if I asked you to turn into a mouse right now, you wouldn't be able to do it?"

Keleon smiled.

"That's correct. Although I'm not sure why you'd ever want me to be a mouse."

My head had never felt so jumbled. The tears had slowed down, but not stopped. The knot in my stomach was still tight, but the anger had dissipated somewhat. I wanted to understand. I needed to understand.

I'd heard of shapeshifters in stories when I was young. Were the stories exaggerated? I didn't know anybody who'd ever seen one, and most people believed they were a myth. There were still more questions I needed to ask.

"When we needed to get the disrupter module, you changed into a Kikorangi girl to get the best deal," I challenged. "That looked pretty deliberate to me."

"I can see why it might appear deliberate," he replied carefully. "I guess it's a bit like you breathing, or blinking. You don't think about doing those things, they just happen. Your body knows what it needs on some subconscious level and just does it. In a similar way, my body knows what appearance to use that would be most beneficial to my circumstances, and just does it. The meditation I do helps with that. Some of my kind believe that we have an extra-sensory perception, some kind of subliminal intuition, that means we can pick up on the subconscious thoughts of others and use them to best suit our immediate environment. Our 'instincts.' I might appear as your most trusted ally, or your greatest fear. I usually don't know until it's already happened. In order to get you out of that facility you were being held in, I guess my intuition told me that the highest priority was that I needed you to come with me voluntarily, so I probably appeared to you as someone you'd be the most inclined to follow."

My head was spinning.

"But now I know it's all an illusion." I could hear the sadness in my own voice as my dream was still shattering around me.

"You make it sound like some kind of deception," he responded. "There was no intent to trick you. My body just decides on the best form to take on its own. It's not an illusion – it's just what I look like right now. Just like that's what you look like right now, and you'll change over time too. I just change shape on a different timescale to you."

Keleon held my hand tighter in his own. We sat in silence while I tried to process what he was telling me. It was all very logical, and I couldn't fault his explanation or reasoning. But it didn't stop the hurt, and I still couldn't hold back the tears.

"Hey," Keleon started again after a little while. "I don't want you to think I've tried to mislead you in some way. From my perspective, I've just been doing what you would consider breathing and blinking, without thinking too much about it. Nothing has changed for me. I still like you, and I still like kissing you. And I still want to be your boyfriend."

My boyfriend.

My boyfriend.

The words turned over in my head until they started to sound strange.

The question was, did I still want this relationship, knowing he wasn't human?

"It's a lot for me to think about," I managed. And then I had another thought. "Is boyfriend the right word? Are you even male?"

"Vacillators don't have genders. The concept of male and female is relatively foreign to me. It's something I'm still getting used to."

"Which is why you have no preference? Why I thought you were pansexual?"

"As I said before, gender doesn't mean anything to me," he reminded me. "But I've become accustomed to you considering me to be male and referring to me as male. In this form, my body has human male organs. As such, boyfriend seems like the most logical description."

We sat in silence for a bit longer while I tried to process what he said. Keleon broke the silence first.

"Are you OK?"

Ever caring, his voice was full of concern. He seemed to understand that I was finding this difficult, even if he didn't know why. I could see he was trying to help me. I owed him honesty.

So, the question was, was I OK?

"I don't know Keleon," I ventured. "I don't know. You're not human? It's a lot to take in. I need to think."

"OK," he replied sadly. "I need to start getting ready for landing on Epsilon 4 anyway."

Keleon was hurt. I could hear it in his tone. Nevertheless, he buckled up and started focusing on flying the ship, leaving me to think as requested. Now that I was over the initial shock, and no longer felt like vomiting, I rested my head on the back of the chair and stared at the ceiling. Tears still rolled towards my ears when I blinked, and I just let them come. I was aware of Keleon talking to Mia remotely about opening the hatch and landing, but their conversation seemed distant. Thoughts swirled round my head like smoke, dissipating almost as quickly as they came; I couldn't hold onto any of them for long. I recognised that on a practical level we'd achieved what we set out to do today, and I probably should have been happy.

But when I adjusted my head slightly so that I could see Keleon, I felt numb.

I knew I had to start accepting that I'd fallen head-over-heels for someone who didn't really exist.

Chapter 14 - The Distraction

I'd been sitting alone on the space craft for about half an hour, and still didn't feel like moving.

Keleon had docked the craft, and had asked whether I needed anything, but I'd just shaken my head and asked to be left alone for a bit. He had obliged and disappeared from the ship, leaving me on my own to think. I hadn't come to any conclusions about anything, though. I'd tried sifting through the information, the emotions, the heartbreak, the internal conflict ... but none of it was helping. I concluded that, although I didn't feel like moving, maybe a walk would help.

As I exited the craft, I caught a glimpse of my reflection in the glass of the window. My hair was a mess and my eyes were red-rimmed. Normally I would have tried to do something to make myself look a bit more presentable, but not today.

I didn't really have a destination in mind as I walked mindlessly through the hanger.

"Damon!" I heard Mia's voice and looked round for her.

She was smiling down from the top of another space craft, with her hair tied back in a messy ginger bun and work overalls covered with oil and grease, with one hand in the air as a greeting. My feet switched direction and started taking me towards her before my brain had caught up with what I was doing. She climbed down her ladder to meet me.

"Hi," she said cheerfully. She must have then registered my tear-stained face, red eyes and unkempt hair, as her smile faded and was replaced by a look of concern. "Are you OK?"

"He's not human," was what tumbled out.

I hadn't intended to talk to her about it, but apparently, that's what I was doing.

"Shit," replied Mia, comprehension appearing in her features. "You didn't know."

It wasn't a question, but I shook my head anyway as I sat on a nearby storage box with my head in my hands. Mia came and sat right next to me. Liquid filled my eyes again. I willed the tears to stop, to no avail, and they fell onto the floor.

"I just assumed you'd had that conversation." she admitted, taking a deep breath. "I guess Keleon thought that information ..."

"Wasn't relevant ..." I finished for her.

We both knew that was what she was going to say.

"And is it?" she asked gently. "Relevant, I mean? You're saying you can't date someone who's not human?"

"I didn't even consider it until a couple of hours ago," I replied honestly. "I just thought he was a bit of an oddball, you know? But he's not who I thought he was, and that hurts so much."

My stomach tightened as I remembered the Kikorangi girl morphing into Keleon in front of me.

"Can you tell me about who you thought he was?" Mia asked. "Aside from his appearance, I mean?" she added, smiling a little.

I thought about the interactions we'd had.

"Well, um, he was very caring. He's made me feel looked after lots of times. He listened when I was upset about him kissing you. He taught me how to fly the craft, and honestly, that was one of the best experiences of my life. We played chess together and it was a lot of fun. He taught me about different types of stars. I even liked his quirks."

"Well, there's nothing you've said there that isn't Keleon," she pointed out. "He can still do all those things without being human."

I knew she had a point, but I was still struggling with it. I decided it was probably because of the feelings of deception. Nobody had intended to deceive me, I was sure, but it didn't stop me feeling like my relationship was a sham. I recognised I was partly angry with myself. I'd assumed too much along the way, only seen what I wanted to see, and not asked enough questions.

Now I had an opportunity to ask things I should have asked before. I sat up and faced her.

"The other day, when you said you liked his 'new look,' you weren't talking about his clothes, were you?" I ventured, with a layer of extra comprehension.

"No," confirmed Mia. "I meant the attractive human male thing. I knew it was him, though, because we've agreed that he'll initiate contact using my name if he's shifted since we last saw each other."

I ran my hands through my hair until my head rested on my knees, feeling like a prize idiot. I sat up when Mia spoke again.

"Do you know how I met Keleon?" she asked.

"He said it was in casino on Gokk?" I responded.

"It was. I was working there as a game hostess. The casino was jointly run by a human and a Neruvian, so most of the clients were from Earth or Neru, but everyone with something of value to gamble was welcome.

"On this particular night, I was working on the Duplex table, which is a game where two players play against each other. A man entered and sat in one of the seats, waiting for an opponent. It wasn't long before the other seat was taken by one of the most beautiful women I'd ever seen. She had straight black hair that was long enough to sit on, dark skin and eyes like melting chocolate. Her dress was simple, but flattering, and showed off her figure in all the right places. I found it interesting that she'd chosen to drink a Sunbolt, which you can tell from its distinctive orange hue. Nerubians love it, but it's not very palatable for humans, so I clocked it because it was an unusual choice for a human.

"But what was even more interesting was the man's reaction to her. He was absolutely transfixed by this beauty. Naturally, he started flirting. She didn't respond, and just played the game as any other customer would, which only made him flirt harder. He became preoccupied with getting her attention, rather than focusing on the game, so he started to lose. I mean, nobody could deny how attractive she was. But to him ... she was totally irresistible, like a drug. Like she was exactly his type. So much so, that he was willing to keep playing just so he could be near her, even if he was obviously going to lose. At the time, I didn't know who to feel sorrier for. This beautiful lady who was obviously not interested in anything except the game, being pestered like that by someone she'd just met, or the man that was desperately trying to win her affection. But I figured that everything they were doing was by their choice, so I didn't intervene while this lady won game after game.

"My colleague also saw what was going on. She concluded that nobody could have that much luck consistently and reported the lady to our superiors for cheating. They re-ran the close-up footage of the games, but because there was no sleight of hand or manipulation of the discs, they had to let her go with her winnings. Besides, her opponent, when questioned, agreed that he didn't feel she had cheated, so what could they do? It can't really be classed as cheating if the reason you've won is because your opponent couldn't focus, and they chose to continue playing anyway.

"The next night I was working the Duplex table again. A Neruvian female sat down to wait for an opponent, and within a few minutes, a Neruvian male sat down with her to play. He was drinking a Sunbolt, but that's not unusual for Neruvians. I don't know what makes Neruvians attractive to each other, but whatever it is, he had it. Same story as the night before. The female was completely driven to distraction by the male, like she just couldn't resist him. And, like the night before, he showed no interest in her, yet he was all she could focus on. Duplex is a game you need to concentrate on, so she inevitably lost game after game too. This didn't seem like a coincidence to me, and as I watched, I saw the same mannerisms, same body language, same use of words, same character as the night before, so I suspected the Neruvian male was somehow the lady with the long dark hair. But I couldn't work out how. They were different heights to each other and had different skin, hair and eye colour, and none of it looked holographic."

"So, what happened?"

"I stopped the game, took the Neruvian to one side and confronted him quietly. He said his name was Keleon and he had a talent for distracting people while they played. The more we spoke, the more I realised he didn't even know what it was that was distracting his opponents, he just knew they weren't paying attention to the game, which gave him a better chance of winning. From his point of view, he was just being himself, playing by the rules and it worked. And in fairness, he never led them on or tried to toy with their affections, he just concentrated on what he was doing and let them fawn over him if they wanted."

"Sounds like Keleon," I conceded, nodding slightly. I noticed I was no longer crying at least. "He said something about being able to instinctively pick up on the subconscious desires of others. Is that how he knew what would distract them?" My face heated up. "What would distract me?" I asked, embarrassed, while Mia nodded. "God, I spent so much time in that facility dreaming about a knight in shining armour, I should have realised it was too good to be true when one showed up that was perfect for me."

"But not a coincidence. It wouldn't have mattered who you were looking for to get you out of there. Keleon would have been it. He can somehow get into the subconscious of his target and he can become their deepest desire. So, if you wanted to be rescued by a beautiful red-headed woman," Mia started twirling her hair and looking innocently up to the ceiling, gesticulating at herself as she did so, "then that's what you would have got. Keleon's low-level telepathy would have morphed him into whatever your heart craved, if that's what suited his purpose. He needed to be the person that was most likely to get you to follow him, so he must have made himself irresistible to you. And now, it seems, your ultimate fantasy man is walking around for everyone to see."

I groaned with humiliation.

"Oh God, don't say that. I feel like such an idiot."

"Please don't. You have an excellent imagination."

I gave her a playful shove.

"You know what I mean. He tricked them both in the casino, and now I've fallen for it too." As I said it out loud, I realise how true that was.

'Driven to distraction.'

'Totally irresistible, like a drug.'

What Mia had described in those other humanoids ... I'd felt those things too. I hadn't paid attention to things I should have focused on because I was trying to capture his interest.

Duped, just like those Duplex opponents.

Chapter 15 - The Black Sheep

"You're not the first person to fall for him, and I suspect you won't be the last," Mia assured me as we continued our conversation while sitting on the storage boxes in the hanger. "But if it helps, as far as I can tell, you are the first one he's fallen for. I haven't seen him reciprocate before. I didn't even know he could."

That got my attention. Mia had just managed to address a concern I didn't realise I had. One of the things I'd believed once we'd started our relationship was that he liked me back, the same way I liked him. And somewhere in those smoky thoughts that I hadn't quite been able to keep hold of, was the question of whether those feelings had been fake. How much of what I'd experienced had been simulated? Just the exterior, or the emotions too?

"How can you tell whether he actually likes me?" I questioned, recognising this was something I needed to know. "He might have kissed me back because he thought it was some human custom, rather than because he actually wants a relationship with me. He doesn't talk about his feelings much."

"He doesn't, but that doesn't mean they're not there. You'll just have to take his word for it. Trust is part of building a relationship," she pointed out. "But if you want my opinion, I do think he likes you the way you want him to."

"What makes you say that?"

"Has he told you he has no conscious control over his shifts?"

"Yeah," I nodded in response to that, remembering his comment about turning into a mouse.

"As far as I understand it, Vacillators shift intuitively, according to what is likely to give them the best outcome," she explained. "They don't have a set form that they go back to because it requires effort for them to shift. A bit like it take effort for your heart to pump blood around your body. It needs to be efficient, and it's not efficient for them to change their appearance if there's no perceived benefit. So, once a particular form has served its purpose, they just stay in it until the next time there's a perceived advantage to shifting."

"OK," I said, not really feeling like she was answering the question. Or maybe she was trying to tell me something and I wasn't grasping it. Either way, I was sure I looked confused.

"So, what does Keleon currently look like? Is he still looking like a Kikorangi, or is he looking like your human boyfriend?" she asked.

"He looked human when we landed," I replied.

"Can't you see? If Keleon was behaving 'normally,' he'd still have blue skin. He must have had a reason to shift back to this human form." Mia smiled gently and took my hand in hers.

"Are you saying he shifted back for my benefit?"

"Sort of, although it won't have been done on a conscious level. Vacillators are like a form of advanced chameleon, which adapts to its surroundings to help it blend in. It's not deliberate, they just do it; it's an instinct that's built into them. The meditation they do, helps them 'tune in' to their surroundings and helps their subconscious make better decisions. When he came to get you out of that research facility, his sole purpose was to get you to follow him out of there. So, he took on a form that best suited his purpose.

"Now that you're out of there, what's the point in shifting back to that form again? It's not like he's trying to get you to follow him or win a Duplex game. I've never seen that happen before, Damon. Some part of him must have realised that you liked the way he looked, and he liked the outcome of that. I guess you could think of it a bit like a peacock, which fans its tail to get the attention of the peahen. The peacock doesn't understand what it's doing, it just sees the peahen and uses its tail feathers to try to attract her. I think he's fanning his tail for you, and it's not for any purpose other than he's trying to get your attention. So, the fact that he changed back after your trip to the blue planet could be interpreted as a compliment rather than an attempt at deception."

"So, I'm a peahen?" I laughed lightly. "And this is his way of flirting with me?"

The irony of the role reversal was somewhat amusing. Now it seemed he was the one flirting, and I was the one being oblivious to it.

Mia smiled reassuringly. "I don't know for sure that that's what's happening, but knowing Keleon, it seems like the most likely explanation. If you decide to pursue a relationship, it will probably be more challenging than a relationship with a human, but honestly, I think you're handling it all remarkably well. If you want my opinion, I think you should give it a go and see how you get on.

"There are some advantages to it, you know. If he ever decides he's no longer interested in you, you'll know, because I suspect he won't look like your fantasy anymore." She squeezed my hand lightly before continuing. "And, you know, there must be some advantages to having a boyfriend that can change his shape to give the best outcome."

Mia wiggled her eyebrows suggestively. I pulled my hands away and pushed her lightly.

"You have a dirty mind."

She pushed me back teasingly.

"You know I'm right."

Talking to Mia was helping. My head felt like it was processing my thoughts better. The more I found out about Keleon, the easier it was becoming to sort out my emotions. I wanted to find out more, as I felt it would lead me closer to finding some resolution.

But how do you know which questions to ask about an alien species, unless you already at least partially know the answers? So, I asked the most sensible thing I could think of.

"I don't know anything about Vacillators," I confessed. "What else can you tell me?"

"Well, um, if you guys ever get married, don't use gold wedding rings," she said.

Out of all the things I thought she might say, that wasn't anywhere near top of my list.

"Why not?"

"I guess it's something like an allergy they have. It doesn't hurt for Vacillators to be in contact with gold, but it does prevent them from shifting. It's the most malleable metal, so kind of fitting for a shapeshifter to have a connection to it. My limited understanding is that if any part of their body is forcibly removed while they're in contact with gold, they'll die."

"OK, no gold rings," I said. "Although, we're only just getting to know each other, so marriage isn't on my mind. And we're probably a bit young to be thinking about stuff like weddings anyway." There was a slight pause as I thought of something else. "Come to think of it, I don't even know how old Keleon is."

"We think he's probably about seven Earth years old," replied Mia.

Shocked, I shot up to a standing position.

I was not expecting that answer.

"Seven?!?!" My outcry echoed throughout the hanger. "What the hell??!" My fingers ran through my hair in distress, and I nearly ripped some of it out in the process. A low rumble rocked through the hanger. This time I knew it was me causing it.

"Hey, Damon, calm down," said Mia quietly, holding out her hand to take mine.

"Calm down?!" I responded, mortified. "Last time I was making out with him, my hands ..." I recalled clearly my fingers slipping into the waistband of his jeans. "Oh God ... I nearly ... Shit! This is so wrong. He's seven?! I thought he was, like, twenty or something!"

The acidic taste of bile rose into my throat.

"Hey, hey," Mia responded in a calm and reassuring tone, gently pulling me back down to sit beside her. "I can see what you're thinking, and you need to stop right there. You can't think about Keleon's age in the same way that you think about human ages. He's not human, remember? He's not a minor, he's an adult, just like you."

"He's an adult?" I repeated as I sat down and looked at Mia.

"Damon," she looked at me seriously. "Do you think I would have been congratulating you guys on an intimate relationship if he wasn't? Keleon is most definitely an adult. Vacillators reach maturity after about five Earth years, so he's two years into adulthood. Which technically means he's been an adult for longer than you have, so thinking of him being around twenty in terms of maturity isn't actually far off."

"But he's not twenty," I argued. "He's seven."

"Why are you getting hung up on a number that really only applies to humans?" she asked. "Even if you just look at Earth, different species mature at different rates. Most animals on Earth mature before they get to eighteen years, and for many of them their lifespans are far less. If every animal had to wait until they were eighteen Earth years old before they could propagate, most of them would be extinct. If anything, humans are the abnormal ones. Taking eighteen years to get from birth to adulthood is not normal for most species. I'm not just talking about Earth, but on other planets too."

I sat in silence, letting the information sink in. She had a good point; there was no point in comparing his growth rate to mine when we weren't the same species. I took a deep breath and released it. I had to focus on the fact that where he came from, he was fully-grown.

"Better?" Mia asked, and I nodded. "I promise Keleon is an adult, Damon. I would have stepped in and stopped your relationship if he hadn't reached maturity. If the two of you decide to be together, I don't see anything wrong with it from an age perspective, and neither should you."

"OK, I get it," I replied honestly. "You're right. If we're going to continue being together, I need to stop thinking of him as a human. Age included." I took another deep breath. "So how long have you been travelling together?"

"He left his home as soon as he was an adult," she replied. "Most Vacillators don't want to leave their home world, which is why there aren't many of them around and a lot of people think the stories about them are legends. So, he's different from most of his kind. He's quite sociable, where most of them aren't. He left to go exploring, find out what else was out here and have new experiences. When I found him on Gokk, he'd been travelling for about six months already, and we've been partners for about eighteen months now."

"That's what he meant by black sheep," I remembered the phrase he used to describe his relationship with his family. "So, is there anything else? Like is Keleon really his name?"

"Good question," she replied. "The name Keleon was given to him by one of the first humans he met, as humans can't make the correct sounds to say his name in his language. The human actually called him "Chameleon," but he thought that was too long and wanted to shorten it."

"OK, so Keleon is essentially short for Chameleon," I reiterated. "That would have been helpful to know earlier," I added, more to myself than to Mia. "You said earlier he was drinking Sunbolts. Does that mean he likes them?"

Mia gave me a smile. "He does, yeah. Keleon doesn't need to eat, sleep or even breathe. He can simulate all of them though. Sometimes he does it to fit in, and sometimes does it because he likes the sensation. And apparently, he does actually like Sunbolts. Having them on Gokk helped him seem more humanoid, but he also likes the sensation of what they taste like to him."

I tried to think whether I'd ever seem Keleon eat or sleep. I realised I hadn't.

And it wasn't the only thing I realised. Mia must have spotted the change in my expression.

"You OK?" she prompted.

"Shit," came my response. "When we were on the Pavo together, he was trying to share who he was with me. I asked him if he needed to sleep, and when he said he didn't, I just thought he meant he wasn't tired. But now I'm thinking about the way he answered the question from his point of view – he was literally telling me he didn't need to sleep. Like, at all. Same with eating. When he said he didn't need food, I assumed he meant he wasn't hungry at that time. And there were lots of other times where I thought he was just saying weird stuff. But he wasn't, he was trying to help me to understand him better."

"Do you know how attractive you are to me?"

"I guess sometimes it works that way. But nobody's had this reaction to me before."

My hands were pushing back through my hair in frustration again.

"Jesus Christ, Mia, how have I been so stupid?"

"Keleon can be very convincing. And very distracting."

"Yeah, I got that." I rested my head on my knees as guilt crept over me. "Fuck. I've messed this whole thing up."

"Really? How were things left between you?" Mia asked gently.

"I told him I wasn't sure about continuing our relationship," I admitted.

"And now that you've had a chance to get more information and talk it through?" she asked. "Do you still feel that way?"

I shook my head slowly.

"I don't think so," I replied. "I was angry with Keleon for tricking me, like everything we shared together had been a lie." I sighed heavily. "But now I can see it from the other side. And actually ... there were so many things he was telling me, and I just wasn't paying attention. I didn't listen hard enough. I made assumptions, and I didn't stop to question them or check them out, even when it was obvious that I should have. It wasn't fair for me to have put the blame on him." I ran my hands through my hair and looked straight into her eyes as a wave of comprehension hit me. "Shit. I really like him, Mia."

"You can still make it right," she said sympathetically.

"Only if he forgives me," I fretted.

"He's not the type to hold a grudge," Mia put a hand on my arm. "Although there may be certain things you need to make really clear if you're going to talk to him about it."

"Yeah, I know," I responded, knowing what I had to do next. I gave her a quick peck on the cheek. "Thanks Mia. You're a star."

"I'm glad it helped," she replied.

I pushed myself off the storage box.

"Wish me luck," I said, as butterflies danced in my tummy. "I need to go and sort this out with Keleon."

Chapter 16 - The Peacock

I was much calmer as I walked through the hanger, away from Mia and towards Keleon's room.

Talking to Mia had helped me to understand Keleon better. It helped that I'd had some time to recover from the initial shock of my earlier discovery. Keleon wasn't who I thought he was, but I had concluded that that wasn't a good reason to discontinue what we had.

What he'd looked like in the beginning had had an influence on me, of course, but was that what mattered in a partner? If I were to list the qualities I'd want in my boyfriend, they would include honesty, kindness and reliability. Someone who would do their best to be a team with me. I had someone like that, and I needed to appreciate that, rather than which planet they happened to be born on, or whether they looked a certain way all the time. I needed to stop being so shallow and start making this right.

I knocked softly on Keleon's door, and when there was no answer, I knocked a little louder.

"Keleon?" I called, but there was no response.

I opened the door enough to put my head round, and then wider when I couldn't see him. He wasn't there. Disappointed, I closed it behind me and walked down the small corridor back to my room. Helen walked around the corner as I approached my door.

"Damon," she said cheerily. "Keleon gave me the disrupter module, and I was just coming to catch up with you about it."

"Um, can it wait a little bit?" I asked. "I actually need to find Keleon. Do you know where he is?"

"Sure, it can wait, no problem," Helen smiled. "I saw him go outside." She pointed to the northwest hanger door.

"Thanks, Helen," I said, kissing her on the cheek. "I'll catch up with you later!"

I jogged towards the door and made my way down the little path that Keleon and I had followed before, leading north of the hanger. The air was just as crisp as it had been the last time I'd come down here, and I slowed down and picked a couple of the orange fruits that were hanging from the bushes and snacked on them while I made my way down the worn path.

I arrived near the water and gently parted the vegetation so I could look around. The scene looked somewhat familiar, the two moons glowing a pretty pink in the early evening sun. I turned my gaze to the mossy bank where Keleon and I had been together before. The person meditating on the mossy bank was wearing a shimmering aqua-blue outfit, 'her' long green hair spilling down the sides of it. 'Her' eyes were closed, but I knew they'd be deep blue if they opened.

My heart sank and my stomach twisted. Not because of what Keleon looked like, but because of what it implied. There were limited reasons why he would shift into a Kikorangi girl, and none of them looked good for me.

"If he ever decides he's no longer interested in you, you'll know, because I suspect he won't look like your fantasy anymore."

Shit, I hoped I hadn't messed this up beyond repair. I knew now that it took effort to shift, and apparently Keleon had reason to make that effort. I hadn't even made contact and it felt like I'd been rejected already.

I walked so that I was close by, but quietly so that I didn't disturb 'her.'

"Damon."

'She' opened her deep blue eyes. I supposed Vacillators must have good hearing.

"Sorry, you're meditating. Am I interrupting?"

"No, I can take a break if you need something."

Keleon's posture changed as 'her' focus shifted to me.

"I've had some time to think," I ventured.

"Yeah. Me too," 'she' replied a little stiffly.

"I can see that," I responded gently, indicating I'd noticed Keleon's change of appearance. "Mind if I sit with you?"

"Go ahead."

I sat opposite the Kikorangi girl, trying to read 'her' emotions from her expression. I wasn't well versed in Kikorangi facial expressions, but 'she' definitely wasn't smiling.

"Any idea why you've shifted?" I asked.

I reached forward to touch 'her' face as I asked the question. I wasn't sure why. Maybe I wanted to feel a physical connection. Maybe I wanted to comfort 'her.' Maybe I wanted to demonstrate that any hurt or anger I'd had earlier, had now dissipated.

Regardless of my intentions, Keleon flinched backwards slightly, away from my incoming hand, and my stomach twisted tighter. No touching, then. I pulled my hand back in and put it in my lap with the other one.

"No," 'she' replied. "I'm not choosing it. My best guess is that it will make it easier for you to terminate our agreement."

I knew Keleon could pick up on my subconscious, although not on a level 'she' could consciously recognise. So that couldn't be the reason Keleon had shifted, because part of 'her' must know I wasn't here to break up. There had to be another reason.

"Or maybe you're pushing me away," I suggested. "Humans sometimes do that if they get hurt. To stop themselves getting more hurt."

"But I'm not human," 'she' reasoned.

"Maybe you're more human than we thought," I said, offering a small smile. I shuffled a little bit closer. "Look, I don't want to 'terminate' anything, OK? That's not why I'm here."

"You didn't exactly look happy when I last saw you," Keleon pointed out. "I know it was because of what I am. You liked me before you realised I was a shapeshifter. I can see now that what I look like may be important to you. And I have no control over it."

"And you think I won't like you if you don't look like the human male?" I guessed. "And because you can't control what you look like, you're pushing me away so that it doesn't hurt as much if your body decides to shift and I don't like it."

"It's difficult to interpret your actions any other way," Keleon pointed out. "You didn't react well to finding out I could change my appearance."

"And you think I might not react well if it happens again?" I asked, and 'she' nodded.

"When you've been angry and I don't know why, or what to do, I can't describe how awful that feels," Keleon explained.

"You're right. I didn't react well, did I?" I acknowledged. I moved to take 'her' hand in mine, and then remembered that 'she' may not want physical contact right now and pulled back. "I'm so sorry for that. I didn't even know what I was reacting to, so it's no wonder you were confused. But I've had some time to think. Now I know I wasn't upset because of what you are. I was upset because I didn't understand what you are. And I also know that getting upset wasn't the right way of dealing with the confusion I had."

Keleon didn't look convinced.

"I'm an emotional person, even by human standards," I continued. "I have a hot temper that flares up quite easily and can get upset at things I don't understand. But it doesn't normally last too long, and if I've done something wrong, I'll always try to make it right. It works the other way too; little things can make me happy. You've made me happy.

"I know my emotions might make me seem hot and cold sometimes. When I first found out you could shift, I wasn't feeling disgust, it was shock; I just wasn't expecting anything like that because I was so convinced you were human. It wasn't fair for me to get upset with you, and I hope you'll accept my apology for that."

Keleon paused for a minute, presumably processing what I'd said, and then nodded awkwardly. I hoped that meant my apology was accepted, and 'she' just wasn't sure what to do next.

I decided to go with that assumption.

"Thank you," I smiled, but I knew there was still more that needed to be resolved. "I guess we probably need to decide what we're doing about our relationship now," I ventured. "I'd still like you to be my special person, if you'll have me. Only this time we would both know more about what we're getting into."

Silence followed. I wasn't sure what that meant, so I decided to keep talking.

"I know it might be hard for you to accept my variable emotions. I guess you need to decide for yourself whether the highs are worth the lows. For my part, I'll work on taming my temper, because I never wanted to hurt you, and I don't want to hurt you again."

I waited for some kind of response, caught somewhere between hope and heartbreak. It was only a few seconds, but it felt like minutes.

"So ... what I look like isn't important?" Keleon broke the silence. "Or, whether I'm human or not?"

I reached out slowly to take 'her' hand again, and when 'she' didn't flinch, I took it gently.

"OK, so, this is how I see it. Some days you'll look male, some days you'll look female. There will be some days you won't even look human. I've accepted that, and I'm OK with it. I'm ready to look past the physical aspects and see the person inside. Because that person has taught me about the stars and taught me how to fly through them. That person has taught me that friendships and bonds can blossom despite huge differences in culture and even biology. That person has taught me about the importance of listening and communicating on levels I'd never imagined before. That person made me take a good hard look at myself and made me realise what really matters to me.

"In the beginning, I thought I was teaching you about relationships, and in the end, it's you that has taught me. Your appearance may have been what initially attracted me to you, but I promise you Keleon, that's not what's keeping me here now."

As I looked into the deep blue eyes that were mirroring my gaze, I realised the truth in my own words. What I was seeing in front of me wasn't a Kikorangi girl. It was Keleon. With blue skin and long green hair, yes, but it was still Keleon. Someone I felt a connection to, running deeper than what 'she' looked like.

I didn't realise I was so close to 'her' face until my mouth was about an inch from 'hers.' But 'she' hadn't flinched back this time or moved away. I never thought I would voluntarily kiss a girl, or a blue alien, but apparently, I was about to kiss someone that appeared to be both because I wanted to. Because my feelings for this person, irrespective of their gender or species, were too deep for it to matter anymore.

I looked down at Keleon's lips and they parted slightly; an invitation for me to continue. When we connected, it was as light as a feather, our lips barely touching at all. I moved my mouth slightly so that I could feel more of the delicate link between us. Still, Keleon didn't move, so I ran my tongue gently over 'her' lower lip and caught the familiar taste of cherries. I heard a noise that sounded like a whimper, which spurred me to press a little harder and let my tongue explore a little further. This time Keleon kissed me back. I felt 'her' tongue reaching for mine; a welcome sign that 'she' was connecting with me.

My hand slipped out of Keleon's hand, and round to the back of 'her' head, with the intention of deepening the kiss. I was expecting to feel long hair, but instead I felt short hair.

I automatically moved away to ascertain what had happened, and I found myself looking into the crystal ocean-blue eyes of the human male that had pulled me out of the facility on Selenia.

"You're back," I whispered, confused. "Why have you shifted back? I told you it didn't matter anymore."

Before he had a chance to respond, my heart tripped over itself with comprehension, and I grinned involuntarily.

"You're being a peacock," I said, pushing his hair back out of his eyes, knowing it would flop back down as soon as I pushed back far enough. "Fanning your tail." I pecked him on the lips.

I understood now. He'd shifted to a Kikorangi girl, a form that he felt I would reject, because on some subconscious level he needed to see how much appearance mattered to me. He needed to know that his shapeshifting was OK before he could flirt with me again. Now that he was convinced that I liked him regardless, he felt comfortable enough to fan his tail.

And I loved it. Not because he looked hot (although that certainly didn't hurt), but because of the message it was sending me; I knew now that it was his way of trying to attract me. To let me know he wanted me too.

"You know you still don't make sense to me sometimes," Keleon interrupted my thoughts. "What's a peacock?"

"It doesn't matter," I grinned. "Take it as a compliment. I like peacocks."

Chapter 17 - The Decision

"You're so odd, Damon," he replied, cocking his head slightly after my peacock comment. "But I like you."

"So, does this mean we're back on?" I asked. His appearance already told me the answer, but I think we both needed it to be said. "Do you still want to be my boyfriend?"

"I'm willing to try and see what happens," he nodded.

I felt his hand creep into my hair, just as I was about to let him know that I was glad he thought we could try again. Gently, he tugged my face forward to close the small gap between us, and he swallowed my words with his mouth on mine. The only sound that managed to escape me was a hum as I complied with his silent request. Without breaking the kiss, I slowly repositioned myself so that I was sitting in his lap with my legs wrapped round him and my arms round his neck. One of his hands stayed in my hair and one snaked round my waist as the kissing got heavier. I rocked against him, moving from my waist, feeling dizzy with passion when he mirrored the action.

The amazing feeling of soaring started to take over again, and that's when I felt it. Gravity. Or rather, lack of gravity. It was like having an extra sense;

I couldn't taste, smell, touch, see or hear it, but I felt it. We were about to leave the ground, but this time, I didn't stop what we were doing.

Keleon was oblivious to everything except us, and although I wanted to be there as well, part of my focus needed to be on making sure neither of us got injured through falling. I moved my mouth away from his, so that I could at least partly focus on this new 'gravity' sense, and I kissed along his jaw to just below his ear. I gripped the back of his head with my hands and used my mouth on his neck, rocking myself against him as I did. It still felt great for me, but with my mouth away from his, I could focus on not mixing these feelings of lust with the gravity sense. Lust – or rather, getting lost in it – was what triggered the floating. I understood now that I could actively feel it. I guess being able to focus fully on Keleon would require practice at separating the two senses, so for now, I would practice. And hopefully make him feel good in the process. I worked my way back up his neck passionately, still gripping the back of his head.

Apparently, my attempts multi-tasking didn't stop him being fully focused on me.

"Damon," he breathed, with his head tilted back and his eyes closed.

"You OK?" I said gently, right next to his ear as I nibbled it gently.

Keleon was relaxed in my arms, lips parted slightly.

"More than OK," he mumbled. "It's ... "

The next kiss I gave him involved my teeth lightly scraping across his neck, and the action caused his sentence to deteriorate into a throaty noise.

I loved that noise he made. I nearly lost control, and then remembered I needed to concentrate on what I was doing before we found ourselves in the air.

"You're not going to finish the sentence?" I teased as I squirmed in his lap. Rubbing against him made my groin ache, and it felt nice. I closed my eyes and made sure everything around me was tethered to the ground, including us. I kissed my way round the bottom of his neck, to the other side, and kissed him long and hard just below his other ear.

"Do you know ... what that's ... doing ... "

Keleon cut himself off, groaning and holding me into his lap tightly as I scraped my teeth lightly along this side of his neck.

The noises he made were delicious. The way he pulled me into his body turned me on in ways I'd never imagined. I reluctantly forced myself back to reality, reigned in the lust a little bit, closed my eyes and checked we were safely attached to the surface of the planet.

"I have a fairly good idea," I grinned against his neck, excited that I could have this effect on him.

The whole thing reminded me of trying to pat my head and rub my tummy at the same time when I was a kid. It was difficult at first, but with a bit of practice, I was convinced I'd probably be able to do this a bit more naturally, and hopefully be able to get as lost in the sensations as my boyfriend was, without causing us to hover above the ground in the process.

I smiled as he whimpered under my touch, and I decided that in the meantime, giving Keleon pleasure had its own rewards. Not just the amazing sounds he was making, or that I could feel how hard he was through our clothes, but the expression on his face was quite possibly one of the sexiest things I'd ever seen.

My hands and lips kept exploring while I practiced the self-control and coordination of my new skill.

And then my stomach growled with hunger.

Keleon stopped abruptly and looked towards the noise.

"You're hungry," he concluded.

"I'm not," I protested.

I moved in to kiss him again, but his hand stopped me.

"When was the last time you ate?" he asked.

"I grabbed some of those orange fruits on the way here. I'm fine," I reassured him, trying to get back to kissing him.

Unfortunately, my stomach growled again, as if it were arguing against me. I mentally willed it to shut the fuck up.

"You haven't eaten properly since before we left for Kikorangi, have you?" Keleon persisted.

I could see I wasn't going to win this one, slipping away from him onto the moss, sighing in defeat.

"Probably not," I grumbled.

Keleon stood up.

"We need to get you something to eat," he said, holding out his hand.

My stomach growled in agreement. As I took his hand and stood up, I noticed that the sun had mostly set now, and the pink glow of the moons had faded somewhat.

"OK," I responded reluctantly.

We started walking, hands interlocked, down the worn path back to the hanger. I grabbed another orange fruit from one of the nearby bushes on the way. They were really quite good.

"So, you don't get hungry, huh?" I asked, taking a mouthful of my snack.

Keleon smiled at me.

"I told you that on the flight back from Selenia."

"Yeah, I remember," I agreed, remembering how I'd interpreted him incorrectly. "Don't you ever eat?"

"There are certain traits I can simulate, or at least that my prevailing body is automatically able to simulate, based on what's expected by my target's subconscious," he explained. "So, I can simulate eating, drinking, breathing and blinking, but I don't need to do any of those things. Breathing and blinking happen automatically because they're functions that the target expects, but not because they're required. Eating and drinking I can choose."

I'd almost finished my orange fruit and was debating whether to pick another one. I decided to wait until we got to the hanger before I had anything else.

"Do you like eating and drinking?" I asked.

"I guess it depends what's on the menu," he replied.

"You like Sunbolts though, right?"

He glanced sideways at me.

"You've been talking to Mia."

"A bit," I confessed with a little grin. "I wanted to understand you better. I still want to understand you better. Is that OK?"

"Of course," he said. "Ask me anything you want to know."

I paused while I tried to think of how to phrase what I wanted to ask.

"So, what we did back there," I nodded behind me. "Were your reactions synthesised, or were you actually enjoying it? I mean, you looked like you were enjoying it."

My face heated up and I could tell I was starting to get a little flustered, so I stopped before I made a total idiot of myself.

"I'm not completely sure how everything works on a technical level," replied Keleon. "My body probably recreated the expected sensations, based on what it picked up from you. But my resulting experience was real. At least, it was real to me." He stopped walking and faced me, taking both my hands in his. "I have no idea whether what I felt back there is what a human would have felt or not. I've never actually been human, so I've got nothing to compare it to. But I can tell you that whatever that was you were doing to me was like nothing I've ever felt before. It was addictive. Stopping to come back and get food was ... difficult."

That told me what I wanted to know.

"I understand. I didn't want to stop either."

I smiled and guided him into the main part of the hanger, and we headed for the food cupboard. Mia was already in there, separating out some of the foods into different bags.

"Hi," she smiled when she saw us. Her smile grew when she noticed our interlocked hands, and her eyebrow lifted a fraction. "You guys OK?" she asked, but I knew she was referring to whether we'd resolved our earlier issues.

"Damon's hungry," replied Keleon, oblivious to the 'real' question.

"You've not eaten?" Mia looked at me, her expression and tone like a mother telling off her child.

"Keleon distracted me," I defended. I knew she'd understand what I meant after our previous discussion.

"That's not entirely true," Keleon corrected me. "You also distracted me. Especially when you..."

"OK, I don't think Mia needs all the details," I interrupted, my face heating up again.

"Yeah, I got the idea," agreed Mia, smirking. "I'm just sorting food to take with us tomorrow to Selenia. Are you happy to grab what you need from round me?"

"We're going tomorrow?" I asked, letting go of Keleon's hand to take a couple of the ration packs and a bottle of water.

"Not you, Damon," she replied. "The rest of us are going. You're staying here."

"I want to go with you."

"You're the one they want, Damon. It's too risky," insisted Mia.

"But I can help," I protested. "I know my way around the building."

"There's no way you're going inside that building," replied Mia.

"Then let me come and stay in the ship," I said.

I couldn't stay on this planet while they went to get Mum, it would drive me insane.

Mia paused while she sorted more food into bags.

"I suggest you talk to Helen in the morning," she responded. "She's gone to bed to get some rest before tomorrow," she continued. "In the meantime, I suggest you do the same."

"OK, thanks Mia," I smiled at her. I grabbed a couple more of the packs and some fruit, before heading towards my storage room. I was delighted when Keleon exited with me and came into my room as if he belonged there. As far as I was concerned, he did. We sat on the blankets together while I ate.

"I'm not sure you should come tomorrow," he said. "I'm worried about your safety."

"And I'm worried about yours," I replied.

"I'm not the one they want," he countered. "They're unlikely to fall for the same trick twice. They must have realised a shapeshifter was involved in your disappearance last time. I took on different forms throughout the building, so presumably they got some interesting security footage."

"All for whatever it is that's in my blood," I shook my head, and opened another pack.

"Talking of which," Keleon continued, "I expected the kissing we did down by the water to have lifted us into the air again. I didn't think about it at the time because ... well ... I wasn't thinking about much at all." I knew that but grinned anyway. "Now that I am thinking about it, shouldn't that have triggered a gravitational distortion?"

"It kind of did," I replied between mouthfuls. "But I felt it and managed to counter it."

"You can control it?" Keleon sounded excited.

"I wouldn't go that far. I can feel it. And if I focus, I can do enough to stop things floating," I explained, finishing my mouthful. "It was the first time I felt it properly, down by the water, and it's hard to explain what it was like. I just kind of knew it was there and could feel how to temper it." I finished my food and cleared up my mess.

"That's pretty cool," remarked Keleon. "Do you think you can control it the other way? When you're feeling angry or upset?"

"No idea," I replied, downing some water. "I guess the only way to find out is the next time I'm angry or upset. Are you planning to upset me?" I teased, crawling over to him.

"No," he replied as I pulled myself into his lap and went to resume where we left off before food. His hand stopped me. "But we're not starting that again."

"Well, that's going to upset me," I pouted.

"You need your sleep."

"You have too much self-control," I grumbled.

"On the contrary," he said. "I don't have enough. Besides," he continued. "You have needs that I don't, and we need to make sure they're catered for. If we start this again, I'm unlikely to want to stop."

I sighed at my overly considerate boyfriend. I knew he was right. I'd find it difficult to stop too, and I was feeling tired.

"OK, you win this time," I conceded with a peck on the lips, before pulling away and putting my head in his lap instead, so that I was looking up at him. He started playing with my hair, which I loved, and I wondered whether I might need to think about the effect this might have on gravity again.

"Can I ask you something?" Keleon broke the silence.

"Sure."

"Why did you kiss me the first time? When we played chess, I mean. I haven't had that effect on anyone before and I'm curious."

"You really don't think you've affected anyone like that before?" I asked in response, and he shook his head. "Mia gave me some extra information about the first time you met her," I continued.

"Like the fact that I enjoy drinking Sunbolts?" he queried.

I smiled up at him.

"That was one of the things, yes," I confirmed. "I mean, she gave me more details about how you distracted your opponents by making them want to kiss you."

"What?" Keleon looked shocked. "That's not true. Nobody has ever kissed me before you did."

I chuckled.

"That doesn't mean they weren't trying, Keleon. Other people have reacted like this to you before. It's just that, presumably, nobody else has had enough time or opportunity to act on it or show you. Trapped on a small craft with you for a couple of days gave me time to try my luck."

"Oh," he said, raising his eyebrows.

"Yeah," I said. "It's not your fault you didn't see that. You're young and inexperienced. Maybe by telling you now, it will help you see what's happening next time."

"Inexperienced, maybe," he said, smiling. "But as I understand it, I'm further into adulthood than you are. I believe you've only just reached maturity?"

I sat up and pushed him lightly, smiling back. "You're seven!" I countered.

"Only if we use your arbitrary counting system," he gently shoved me back, laughing.

We descended into banter and giggles after that, and when we calmed down, I brushed my teeth and curled into him with a blanket. I was so glad we were together, and that this time both of us had made the decision with all the relevant information.

Smiling, I drifted to sleep in Keleon's arms.

Chapter 18 - The Plan

I felt the sunlight across my eyes and grumbled as I woke. I concluded that the screen across the window in my room was probably not quite closed properly. I rolled over in the blankets without opening my eyes, hoping that I might be able to go back to sleep if I manoeuvred myself out of the stray rays.

"Morning, sleepyhead," Keleon's voice reached me.

That was enough incentive for me to prise my eyes open and look around.

Keleon was in his meditating position across the room from me.

"You stayed all night?" I asked.

"Not all night," he responded. "I did several checks on the ship once you were asleep, and I also needed to meditate, so I brought my blankets through."

"You didn't meditate in your own room?" I asked, surprised.

"Would you have preferred me to have gone to my own room?" Keleon looked just as surprised.

"No, of course, not, I just thought you'd prefer to be on your own for meditating. I thought you might like some peace, that's all."

"You sleep quietly," he replied, cocking his head slightly and smiling. "And I liked being near you."

My heart stuttered at the words, and I sat up to gather my bearings.

"I liked waking up to you," I confessed. I crawled across to him and into his arms. "It means I get to invade your personal space before I do anything else."

Keleon kissed my forehead.

"My personal space isn't being invaded," he replied. "There's enough room for two. However, we have quite a big day ahead of us, and we're still not sure whether you're coming or not. I suggest we get up and speak to Helen."

"I'm coming with you to Selenia," I said, determined.

I freshened up, fed myself and brushed my teeth, and it wasn't long before Keleon and I were knocking on Helen's door, and she was asking us to enter. Mia was already inside.

"Morning, Helen," I greeted her. "Sorry I didn't get a chance to talk to you last night."

"Damon wants to come with us today," Mia said, starting a discussion in which Helen made it clear she wanted me to stay on Epsilon 4 for my own safety. I explained that I wanted to help, that I'd spent the last three years with people telling me what to do, and now that I was an adult, I wanted to make my own decisions. I also argued that I could be useful; I knew the inside of the building better than anyone else, and that I could fly the Pavo.

In the end, Helen and I compromised, and decided that I should fly with the group to Selenia but stay inside the craft. Knowing that I could fly it, I could take off in a hurry if we needed to.

On the flight to Selenia, Helen explained that everyone would be equipped with several smoke grenades which would help to obscure the vision of the G.I.A. personnel. However, she also pointed out that they would also obscure the vision of the user, so they should be used with caution and only if they gave us an advantage.

She also told us that the disrupter module would knock out all electrical equipment within about a kilometre for about an hour, so there was no reason for anyone to take electrical equipment into the building as it wouldn't work anyway.

Nobody would be taking weapons, for two reasons. Firstly, the G.I.A. weapons were electrical and wouldn't work once the disrupter module was in action. We had the element of surprise, and only the security guards were equipped with weapons anyway, as most of the staff were researchers and wouldn't be armed. But more importantly, we needed to be able to create a legal battle on the other side of this, which we wouldn't be able to do if we severely hurt anyone. They were unlikely to hurt us for the same reasons.

We arrived in the orbit of Selenia faster than it took to go in the opposite direction. I remembered we couldn't use thrusters on our way out so that they couldn't detect us, but nobody was going to be looking for an ion trail in the opposite direction, so we could use the extra speed available to us.

I felt like a bit of a spare wheel as the team worked out the best place to dock so that their plan could be implemented quickly. Each of them had memorised the schematics of the building so that they knew their way around, but nobody knew which part of the building my mother was being held in. So, the plan was to search the building and then to get out and meet back at the ship after an hour, regardless of whether they managed to get Mum out or not.

It was the middle of the night on Selenia as we docked, although now I had adjusted to Epsilon 4, it didn't even feel like lunchtime yet. My aunt reminded me I was to stay in the craft as the team got themselves ready. Keleon kissed me on the forehead as they all stepped out into the darkness, and I fully intended to make sure I was ready to get them out of there quickly if I needed to.

Lost in my own thoughts, after about ten minutes, I remembered something I hadn't thought about for three years. I'd pushed it to the back of my mind because at the time it had seemed inconsequential. Walking through one of the southern corridors with a nurse when I'd first arrived here, there were some storage rooms without forcefields. I'd asked what they were for, and the nurse had told me that the rooms were there in case any of the forcefields ever went down, they still had a place to store things of value. Apparently, it was based on ancient Earth technology. The doors had an old-style "lock and key" mechanism, where a physical key was required to open a physical door. The key would have to be entered into a hole in the door and turned in order for the door to open and close. The security guards were the ones looking after the keys.

If I oversaw security, and there was a breach where the forcefields went down, I would probably move Mum to one of those storage rooms and use this "lock and key" mechanism. But my aunt and her team wouldn't know to look there, and since they hadn't taken radios, I had no way of telling them.

Even if they did find Mum in one of those rooms, they would be unlikely to know they needed to get a key from a security guard, or that they then needed to put it in the hole in the door. Either way, they'd come away empty handed and this whole mission would be for nothing.

I moved towards the door of the craft. Using the southern entrance would bring me close to the storage areas. I may not have any smoke grenades, but I knew the facility very well, since it had been my home for three years. I had a useful skill and information that none of the rest of my team had, and it seemed silly not to use it. There was no time for debating with myself; I had to decide quickly.

I'd know exactly which route to take and where I needed to look once I was in there. Getting to the southern entrance would be a different matter, but I was convinced I had enough information from the conversations on the flight over here to determine how to get to there from where we docked.

Under a dark blanket of stars, I aimed myself in the direction of the G.I.A. premises. I found myself behind a large boulder peeking out at the southern entrance to the compound before I fully registered where I was and what I was planning to do.

Everything was quiet at this end of the building. Presumably most of the personnel had been distracted by the arrival of the others at the northern entrance and gone in that direction to investigate. Adrenaline pumping, I reached the southern entrance and tested the forcefield. As predicted, it was offline, and I could stealth into the building relatively easily. Now I just had to focus on not being spotted.

I tiptoed through the corridors and the labs, checking for signs of life while hiding behind walls and turnings. I could hear distant voices but nothing that sounded close. I was nearly half-way through the southern end of the building when I found the storage rooms I was looking for, in a corridor just off one of the larger laboratories. Each one had a thin window in the door that I could use to look through and see what was inside. Carefully, I peered into the first one, but it was difficult to see anything when it was the middle of the night and the lights were out. My eyes strained against the darkness, but there didn't appear to be anything in there that might be a person.

My eyes were starting to adjust to the very low level of lighting. I scanned the area before moving over to scrutinise the next storage room through its window. Nothing.

I moved back into the nearest alcove.

Maybe this was a bad plan after all.

Chapter 19 - The Reflection

Bad plan or not, I was here now, and it seemed silly not to check the rest of the rooms while I could. Listening for any sign of movement, I crept forward to the next door and slid my eyes up to the window. Scanning the room, I saw a shadow move in the corner. That had to be my mother.

"Mum," I whispered through the keyhole. I got no response. I repeated myself slightly with a more forceful whisper, not daring to speak any louder. "Mum." The shadow moved slightly closer.

"Damon?" Mum's voice came back at me from the other side of the door, not much louder than mine. "What the hell are you doing? You need to get out!"

"Shhh," I responded, as I thought I heard footsteps approaching in the darkness, and I slipped back around into the alcove where I hoped the complete blackness would smother any sign of me. Evidently someone had heard something happening down this way and had come to investigate.

The soft footsteps advanced towards us. They'd definitely heard us then. I could hear my heart thumping and the blood rushing in my ears, and it sounded so loud to me that I silently prayed that the other individual couldn't hear it too. I held my breath when it sounded like the person had stopped outside the door to Mum's room. The situation was far from ideal - they were about three paces away from me and I was trapped in an alcove.

The silence that followed seemed to last an eternity. Cold shivers spread throughout my body and I knew I needed to breathe again soon. I exhaled as quietly as I could before I ran out of oxygen completely, as I knew that otherwise it would result in gasping loudly. I replaced the air in my lungs just as slowly, hoping I wasn't making any noise.

I heard the scout shuffle closer to me, and I instinctively backed away slightly. Only one step, but it was enough that they could have heard it.

"Damon?" a familiar voice hissed through the darkness.

"Keleon?" I whispered back. "How did you find me?"

"Good hearing," he replied, so low I could barely hear it. He whipped himself round and joined me in the alcove. "You were supposed to stay on the ship."

"I remembered something," I explained just as quietly. "These storage rooms have doors rather than forcefields. They need a key. I thought Mum might be put in one of them when the forcefields went down, and she is. Third door from the left. But we'd need to get a key from one of the security guards, and I have no idea how to do that."

"What's a key?" asked Keleon.

"It's a way of locking and unlocking doors that they used to use on Earth a long time ago," I whispered. "It's a piece of metal that needs to be the right shape to fit into the lock."

Saying those words out loud gave me an idea.

"On second thoughts, forget the security guard," I backtracked, taking Keleon by the hand, and quietly moving us over to the door of the room Mum was in. "We don't need a key. We just need something the right shape."

I lifted Keleon's finger to the lock of the door.

"I know you don't have control over your body," I whispered, "but now would be a really good time for a shift."

I hoped that whatever it was that triggered a shift would get itself inside my head and decide that the best outcome would be to allow him to pick the lock. I realised it had worked when I heard him push his finger into the lock and waited, then turned it in the direction I indicated.

The resulting click sounded deafening in the otherwise silent corridor, and the echo didn't do us any favours either.

Why were these manual locks so loud?

I pushed the door open slowly, trying to create as little noise as possible. Unfortunately, the door creaked loudly, and I knew anyone remotely in the area was going to have heard it. I cursed under my breath, and silently wondered whether the G.I.A. personnel had put Mum in a room with a noisy door deliberately so that they'd hear if she got out.

Either way it was too late. Footsteps were coming in our direction from the northern end of the corridor. We needed to move.

"This way!" I hissed as started pulling both Mum and Keleon towards the southern end of the corridor, and into the lab at the end of it. We'd have to cross the lab to another corridor and keep moving quickly to get to the southern entrance.

The natural light from the stars through the large window meant that the lab was lighter than the corridor. As we entered the lab and started to move across it, five silhouetted figures came through the southern entrance, blocking our escape route. Four figures arrived from the northern end of the lab, from the same direction as we'd just come from. The three of us stood close together in the centre of the lab in a defensive position, but my heart sank as I recognised we were surrounded, and the odds weren't in our favour.

"Damon, we just want to help you," said one of the voices from the north end of the room. It was a familiar phrase from the last three years of my life, but I now knew better than to believe it.

I heard a click and then a hissing sound, and within a few seconds, smoke started rising from around our feet. Keleon ducked into it, and I realised he'd let off one of his smoke grenades so that we had some cover at least. Perhaps creating some confusion would help us get out of here. I grabbed Mum's hand and ducked into the dense smoke to join Keleon, but he had already disappeared into the smokescreen. I could only just about make out my mother, so there was no way I'd see him now. I assumed he'd headed south, since that was our best chance of escape, and with smoke tickling my throat, I pulled Mum in that direction with me. The grenade was still hissing which covered a lot of the noise we made. I heard another click from in front of us as another one was released.

A commotion in front of us made me stop suddenly. There were shuffling noises and some sharp intakes of breath. Mum pulled on my arm quietly and, when I followed her guidance, I found myself underneath one of the benches at the south end of the laboratory near the door we needed. We squeezed up together as much as the space would allow and tried to see what was going on through the smoke.

"We've got one of them," a female voice came from the southern end of the lab. My stomach twisted.

Mum was still very much with me, which only left one person they could have.

"Get the gold cuffs on in case it's the shifter," came another voice, male and closer to us this time.

Shit. Keleon was right about them knowing a Vacillator was involved in my previous getaway, and they apparently also knew gold stopped him shifting.

"Already done, sir," the first voice confirmed.

"OK, let's see which one we've got," the male responded, the smoke dissipating now.

This wasn't good. If he had gold handcuffs on him already, he wouldn't be able to slip out of them by shifting.

Panicked and shaky, I watched helplessly from our hiding place as I heard the click of a cigarette lighter.

Through the fading smoke my eyes searched, hoping to see that they'd made a mistake and cuffed one of their own in the confusion that Keleon had created with the grenades. As the flame moved higher and towards the prisoner, I saw him more clearly.

I felt a sharp twist in my gut and involuntarily sucked in a breath, as the figure's profile came into view.

Because the last time I'd seen that face had been as a reflection in a mirror.

Keleon had shifted – and now he looked exactly like me.

Chapter 20 - The Anger

What the hell was Keleon thinking?

Why had he shifted to look like me, instead of one of the G.I.A personnel? Why wasn't he making them believe they'd made a mistake and cuffed one of their own? Was he trying to get captured?

Of course, I partly knew the answer. Keleon wasn't thinking. And that was part of the problem with this entire situation. Whether or not he looked like my identical twin wasn't within his control.

"It's Damon," the female said, talking about Keleon and assuming it was me.

"It certainly looks that way," agreed the male. "But we need to be sure. Until we have proof, we need to stop the others leaving. Get a blood test done on him. Right now. Everyone else needs to prioritise detaining the others until we're certain it's him."

I went rigid and a cold shiver ran through my core. Didn't they know that forcibly removing part of him while he was still touching the gold would kill him? Perhaps that part wasn't common knowledge?

I stared at him intractably through the darkness.

Tell them Keleon.

He was being patted down, presumably to see whether he had weapons on his person. They took the remaining smoke grenades.

Why wasn't he telling them that he wasn't really me?

The G.I.A. lady started guiding him towards the northern entrance. Helplessly, I watched the events unfold, powerless to stop them.

No, no, no! Don't let them do this. Just tell them the truth!

But Keleon wasn't speaking as they marched him across the lab. Three silhouettes aimed for the southern entrance, presumably aiming to block us off if we tried to leave.

A dozen thoughts flashed through my mind in a single instant. Nobody was supposed to get seriously hurt. On either side. Now Keleon's life was in danger. Because of me. He didn't deserve this. I didn't deserve this either. I'd already lost three years of my life to these people under false pretences, and I didn't want to lose anything else to them. Especially not Keleon.

I silently begged them to stop.

They didn't.

Shock and helplessness started turning to anger. They'd stolen three years of my life, and now they were stealing my boyfriend.

A low, now familiar, rumble could be heard through the building. Some of the G.I.A. personnel looked around, confused and concerned.

These same people had invaded my body, taken my blood, and not told me the truth about why. Anger turned to fury. They'd lied to me, tricked me.

Rage bubbled just beneath the surface of my skin. Loose items around the lab started shaking. Glass smashing against the floor caused some of the figures to look in the direction of the sound. Some were still looking warily around the room.

They'd lied to my family. They'd circumvented the legal system.

My jaw clenched, and I removed my hand from Mum's as I could feel them both turning to fists. Dust fell as plaster cracked the ceiling, followed by larger pieces of gypsum as the rumble deepened in line with my mood. Walls shook and fractured, and one of the windows cracked. People were starting to look a little scared.

They'd confined me. They'd used me for their own benefit. It was all so unfair. And now these same people had Keleon, and whether they knew it or not, they were planning to do something that could result in his death.

Heat coursed through me. I needed to stop them. I couldn't stay under this bench any longer and I erupted like a volcano.

"NO!" I exploded as I flew upright.

"Damon," I felt Mum's hand on my arm, trying to pull me back, but I shook her off.

Another window cracked, and more glass smashed. One of the lamps on a nearby table was rattling as the ceiling continued to fall apart. My vision was filled with a red haze. I could feel the gravitational pull in everything around me. And I could feel it was emanating from me, but I couldn't stop it now, even if I wanted to.

"Let him go," I growled aggressively.

Nobody moved. They were looking between the two of us, probably trying to work out which was the 'real' Damon, but also looking around at the gradually disintegrating laboratory.

Their lack of action fuelled my wrath. Any rational thoughts turned to smoke, swirling around me, and dissipating before I could grasp them. I was wrapped in a cloud of emotion. Voices became distant.

The low rumble was getting louder. The rattling and shaking intensified until it was raining plaster and gypsum. The lamp that had been rattling previously exploded, and someone screamed. That got everyone's attention.

One voice broke through the haze.

"Damon." My mother's voice was gentle and full of concern. "You have to calm down sweetheart. If anyone gets hurt, they'll argue you're dangerous and will have a legitimate reason to detain you."

Her hand touched my arm. I didn't shake it off this time, but I couldn't think straight while they were holding Keleon.

"Let. Him. Go." I growled.

Mum must have recognised then why I was unable to calm down.

"All this energy you're feeling," she said calmly. "Can you focus it on freeing your friend? Can you concentrate on breaking the cuffs?"

My gaze moved to the cuffs. Could I do that? I didn't know. I couldn't think properly. I could feel though. I tried what Mum suggested. I may not be able to control the intensity of the gravitational distortions but perhaps I could control which objects they affected. I focussed my attention on the molecules inside the gold cuffs and found that Mum was right. I could feel inside them – the molecular bonds. The room stopped shaking while I found that I could use the gravity around me ...

That was when the cuffs exploded, and the gold shattered to the floor.

Without something tangible to focus on, my energy shook the room again. The walls groaned under the stress of the ceiling, and one of the far windows smashed.

Keleon was free to shift again, but he didn't. Instead, my lookalike used his freed hands to help him leap over the lab bench that was separating us to come and join me.

Nobody stopped him. The G.I.A. personnel were too busy running to the nearest exit, presumably now realising that any attempt to detain us was futile.

But I was rooted to the floor, rage still consuming me. One of the ceiling lights exploded, but now only Mum and Keleon were in the room with me as the building continued to slowly crumble around us.

"Damon, they've gone, honey," Mum's voice was sounding desperate. "Please sweetheart, we need to get you out of here before the building collapses."

Still, I couldn't move. I recognised that Keleon was safe from G.I.A. but I was still angry. What they did to me, what they did to us, was unacceptable. Three years' worth of hurt had been unleashed and was still pouring out of me.

I recognised the face that entered my vision. It was mine. The other Damon cupped my cheeks and, as I watched, Keleon's familiar face replaced it.

"Hey, hey," he said gently. "It's over." Keleon wrapped his arms round me tightly and pulled me into an embrace, with my face resting on his shoulder. The rage started to dissipate as he continued his gentle reassurances and stroked the back of my head.

"We're safe," he reminded me, keeping me tight in his arms. As the anger continued to dissolve, gravity reverted to normal levels and the room stopped reacting to me.

"It's OK, we're safe." Keleon's voice was like silk as his hand continued to work through my hair.

I felt drained, like all my energy had been depleted. Shame and remorse took over and a silent sob racked my body. My legs refused to hold me up any longer, and Keleon supported my weight as I sunk to the floor with him in tow. He held me into his chest as I released my tears into his T-shirt, curling myself into a foetal position in his arms.

"I'm so sorry," I managed, voice cracking.

"It's OK. We're safe," he repeated, as he kissed my forehead. I felt Mum's arm on my back, rubbing, soothing as the tears kept coming.

A short time later, the undamaged lights came on, and some of the damaged ones flickered. I guess this meant that the disrupter had done its job and our hour was up. Still I blubbered into Keleon's T-shirt as he rocked me gently.

It felt like an eternity before my legs had regained enough energy to stand and walk again. Keleon supported my weight as we found the exit and crossed the moon's surface to the Pavo. I was vaguely aware of passing some G.I.A. personnel en route, but nobody approached us, and I didn't pay them much attention. Even with Keleon's help I needed all my concentration to focus on walking.

Keleon helped me through the door to the Pavo. He took me straight to the bed once we boarded the ship, where I collapsed and passed out from exhaustion.

Chapter 21 - The Truth

The next thing I was aware of was a hand repeatedly stroking my forehead and running through my hair. Feeling sluggish, I opened my heavy eyes and tried to focus on the nearest object.

"Hey," Mum's soothing voice filled my ears as she continued the comforting motion on my head. She was sitting next to me on the bed that I'd passed out on, presumably waiting for me to wake up.

"Hey," I croaked back, realising my throat was dry and that my head was thudding slightly. I could see Keleon resting silently against the wall behind her, observing us, but I focused my attention on my mother.

"How are you feeling?" she asked, concern weighing heavily in her tone.

"Tired," I answered, still feeling groggy.

"Do you want to sleep some more?"

I shook my head.

"It's not that kind of tired. It's more like ... drained."

"Can we get you anything? Something to eat?" she asked.

"I could do with a drink," I replied, hoping it might do something for the dryness in my throat.

"I'll get it," Keleon responded quickly, and was already exiting the room by the time Mum thanked him.

"Your friend has barely left this room since we boarded," said Mum in a soft voice once he'd disappeared from view. "I think he likes you."

I smiled weakly.

"We're not just friends, Mum."

She smiled back.

"I suspected as much. I'm pleased for you. He seems nice."

"He is."

"And a Vacillator?"

"Yeah. I always thought they were a myth."

"It's very rare to come across one, which is why many people don't believe they even exist. Most Vacillators never leave their planet," she explained.

"He's different."

"He's hot."

"Mum!"

"Don't tell me you hadn't noticed?" she teased with a smile and a raised eyebrow.

"Oh my God." I rolled my face into part of the pillow and pulled the remaining bit up to cover the rest of my face, which I could feel changing colour.

"Seriously though, I know what it's like to be involved with someone from a different species."

Keleon re-entered the room with a bottle of water. He sat at the end of the bed and passed it to me. I thanked him, and he rested his hand on my leg near my ankle. I was grateful for the contact.

"I used to be part of a research team, specialising in extra-terrestrial life," Mum continued as I sipped my water. "The last research assignment I was given was to a planet called Aderyn, on the far side of the galaxy. The Aderyn people were able to fly, or at least it looks like flying to humans. They're born with an innate ability to alter gravitational strength in their immediate vicinity. I was assigned to bring back a blood sample from one of the inhabitants for trials in genetic modification in humans.

"They were a peaceful people and very welcoming to us. It was our first contact with this species, other than remote communications to set up an introduction, and their hospitality was extraordinary. We couldn't have asked to be treated any better. We asked if we might kindly take a blood sample home with us, but they didn't believe in genetic modification and refused. The offered many other things - food, spices, gemstones - as gifts, but they would not allow us to take their blood.

"My companions and I were all scientists, and completely understood their point of view. They'd given us their answer and didn't want to press the issue. They welcomed us for a few more days, where I took to spending a lot of time with an Aderyn man, Dain'har. It became clear there was a growing attraction between us, and on my last night, we became intimate and agreed to keep it between us. We knew we couldn't be together after that night, but I had no regrets.

"When we returned to Earth, the council claimed that we hadn't pushed hard enough or negotiated enough. We reminded them that we were scientists, and we believed that ethically and morally we needed consent. But they let us all go. It was frustrating to be dismissed, as I liked my job, but I still felt that I'd done the right thing.

"A few weeks later I found out that I was pregnant. I kept the news as quiet as I could because there was only one possible father. If anyone found out he was one of the Aderyn, I knew they would take my baby and start running the tests that Dain'har was so against."

"Which is why you put my father was 'unknown' on my birth certificate," I inferred. Mum nodded. "And why you've never liked hospitals."

"Only when it comes to you," she smiled, still stroking my head. "Had I got there first after your hoverboard accident, I would have taken you somewhere I trusted. I knew a general hospital facility would take a blood sample and realise there was something peculiar about your blood. But they had no way of knowing what the peculiarity was, because there was nothing to compare it to. Hence the endless testing; they had no idea what they were testing for.

"I pretended to be clueless of course, but I suspected they'd bugged every electronic device I encountered, just in case they found out I knew something. I managed to get a note to Helen asking for her help to get you out since I knew they'd be watching me.

"In the meantime, I made every effort to collect as much data as possible when I visited you, from the records they kept at the facility. Some of the scientists there were very protective of the information. But a couple of the more naïve juniors were sympathetic to a concerned mother who wanted to find out more about her son and let me have access to some of the information. Over time, I collected enough small pieces that I could start to build a bigger picture. And your demonstration of power back there, along with the evidence I've collected, means we now have enough proof that they weren't keeping you there on medical grounds."

"But they still have samples of my blood?" I asked.

"I don't know whether you saw the trail of destruction you left behind, but I don't think much survived your wrath," Mum smiled. "If they're left with any uncontaminated blood samples I'll be amazed."

"I destroyed a building," I winced as her words sunk in. "Won't there be repercussions?"

"Not with what we've got against them," Mum replied. "You were threatened, provoked, and still nobody got hurt. I believe we can argue you're not dangerous, even if you did destroy that facility. I know you can't control your gifts yet, but they don't know that. It could have been a lot worse. And I think that legally, they know we have more on them than they do on us. Really, I think we ended up with the best possible outcome."

I finished the water in the bottle.

"Why have we never seen signs of these 'gifts' before?" I wondered.

"Honestly, I have no idea," replied Mum. "It's not something I investigated when I was with the Aderyn, and I didn't want to draw suspicion after you were born by trying to investigate it in retrospect.

"My best guess is that it didn't kick in until your reached physical maturity, and it sounds like it may be linked to your emotions. Every day was predictable when you were on Selenia, so there was no reason for your mood to change much."

"It was boring," I summarised.

"Exactly," replied Mum. "There was nothing to trigger it until you got out."

"So ... my father is out there? On Aderyn?" I asked.

"He is," replied Mum. "I didn't want you to look for him while I was trying to keep you out of harm's way. But now ... I think he'd be delighted to find out he has a son."

I closed my eyes. I wasn't completely human, and my father didn't know I existed. And I had inherited abilities from him that I may or may not be able to control. It was a lot to take in.

Mum lifted my fringe and kissed me on the forehead.

"I'm glad you're OK," she said. "I'm going to get something to eat. If you need me, or if I can get you anything, just send Keleon out to find me. We're looking forward to seeing you when you have enough strength to join us."

I knew she was giving me and Keleon some time to catch up on what had happened.

"Thanks Mum," I replied as she got up. She nodded as she ducked out of the door. Keleon moved up the bed to take her place. I was starting to feel a bit stronger already.

"So ... we're back on Epsilon 4?" I guessed.

"You slept the whole way back, and then some," he grinned, blue eyes and perfect features staring down at me affectionately.

"Helen and Mia?" I asked.

"They're fine," he reassured me. "They were in the northern end of the building. Further away from the epicentre."

I groaned as he reminded me again of the destruction I caused and the fact that I had so little control over it.

"I was so angry with them for what they were about to do to you," I said, wincing at the memory of it. "Why didn't you just tell them you weren't me?"

"Why would telling them have helped?" he countered. "I looked like you, so I doubt anything I said would have stopped them doing a blood test."

He was probably right. Would I have believed him if I were in the position of the G.I.A. personnel? I'd undoubtedly want to be sure either way.

"I meditate to hone my instincts," Keleon continued. "I need to trust that my body will give me the best shape for the situation. I may not always understand or agree with what it's doing, but if my body was telling me that I was supposed to be 'you,' then telling G.I.A. that I wasn't would have undermined whatever it was trying to do to help me. So, I went with it."

He shrugged and kissed my forehead.

"But look what happened," I retorted.

"Yes," he agreed. "Look at what happened. As your mother said, it resulted in the best possible outcome. Apparently, I needed to make sure you were angry enough to show them what you were capable of, but not so angry that you hurt anyone. Along with the evidence your mother collected, they're unlikely to pursue you any further."

"So, you're taking the credit for this?" I asked incredulously.

"Of course."

Typical of my quirky alien boyfriend.

A small chuckle escaped me, followed by a comfortable silence as we smiled at each other. Keleon was the first to break it.

"So, you're not entirely human," Keleon's smile turned mischievous. "Why didn't you tell me?"

I hit him with the pillow, and we descended into giggles.

****

A couple of hours later I was feeling much better, and Keleon and I were walking hand in hand down the path from the north end of the hanger to the waterside, where we knew the sun would set shortly.

Helen, Mia and Mum were already there, with a blanket spread across the moss. In the middle of the blanket were ration packs, local fruits and water. They greeted us warmly when they saw us, and we joined them happily.

"You look so much better, sweetheart," Mum observed.

"Yeah, I'm definitely getting there," I agreed. "We're having a picnic?"

"Why not?" replied Mia. "It's a good spot for it."

Nobody could disagree with that. I started helping myself to some of the food, as Keleon leaned back and watched.

"So Mum, what's next?" I asked after I'd swallowed some of the fruit.

"I haven't had a proper catch-up with Helen for over three years," she replied. "I think we're going to spend some time together. And then, I'm not sure, I haven't decided yet. I need time to adjust to not having to hide my every move." She reached for her water. "What about you? Have you thought about what you want to do?"

"I think I'd like to join these two in exploring what's out there," I replied. Flying a ship had always been my dream and exploring the galaxy with Mia and Keleon sounded perfect to me. "If they're OK with it of course," I added, realising that I hadn't actually asked them how they felt about it.

"Sounds awesome to me," Mia approved. "And I can't see Keleon objecting." She threw a wink in his direction and he grinned. "What about showing Damon that planet we found in the Tetra Prime system? Maybe we should go there first. After all the recent excitement, we probably just need some time to chill out."

"A mini holiday sounds good to me," I agreed.

"Sure, I'm up for that," Keleon concurred. "On a practical note, we borrowed the Pavo from Helen, and we're running out of things to trade. We may need to stop at Gokk first."

"Does that mean I have to watch people flirt with my guy?" I pouted.

"No," replied Keleon. I watched as a lopsided smile formed on his lips. "You can stay outside if you prefer."

I punched him lightly on the arm. The smile grew, showing off his dimple, and I rolled my eyes.

"Any thoughts on what you might do after that?" Mum was smiling at our banter.

"I don't know," I replied. "Mia and Keleon have never been to Aderyn, and I have a father I've never met who may be able to give me some pointers in how to get the gravity thing under control. Maybe we can go there?" I looked towards my new travelling companions.

Keleon nodded, as he kissed me on the head and pulled me closer. Mia smiled and also nodded.

As we continued enjoying the picnic, surrounded by people I considered my family, I realised that my life was about to change for the better.

And I couldn't wait to get started.